BEWARE, DAWN!

Hmmm. I thought fast. Even Alan wouldn't go so far as to make *long-distance* prank calls. And besides, if he was in Stamford, he couldn't have left that letter on the doormat.

"Can I give Alan a message?" asked Mrs Gray. She sounded a little odd, probably because she was wondering why I was being so quiet.

A message? Uh-oh. I wasn't prepared for that. "Um," I said, stalling for time. But I couldn't think of a thing to say. After a couple of seconds that felt like hours, I just hung up. I was so embarrassed! At least I hadn't identified myself.

"Good going, Nancy Drew," I said to myself. "Really slick." I was no closer to identifying Mr X or Mr Nobody than I had been before. The only thing I was sure of was that Mr X and Mr Nobody were the same person. And I was beginning to worry.

BEWARE, DAWN!

Ann M. Martin

Scholastic Children's Books,
Scholastic Publications Ltd,
7-9 Pratt Street, London NW1 0AE

Scholastic Inc.,
555 Broadway, New York, NY 10012-3999,USA

Scholastic Canada Ltd,
123 Newkirk Road, Richmond Hill,
Ontario L4C 3G5, Canada

Ashton Scholastic Pty Ltd,
P O Box 579, Gosford, New South Wales,
Australia

Ashton Scholastic Ltd,
Private Bag 1, Penrose, Auckland,
New Zealand

First published in the US by Scholastic Inc., 1991
First published in the UK by Scholastic Publications Ltd, 1994

ISBN 0 590 55301 1

Typeset in Plantin by Contour Typesetters, Southall, London
Printed by Cox & Wyman Ltd, Reading, Berks.

10 9 8 7 6 5 4 3 2 1

*The author gratefully acknowledges
Ellen Miles
for her help in
preparing this manuscript.*

1st CHAPTER

"Okay, Johnny, see if you can find—let's see—how about this one? The shoe." Johnny bent over the magazine and started to turn its pages quickly, scanning each one for a picture of a shoe.

I was babysitting for the Hobarts that day, and Johnny, the youngest (he's four), and I were busy with his *Highlights* magazine. A lot of the activities in it were too hard for him—the ones that involved reading or spelling—but the "find the picture" game was perfect. He was content to sit on the porch steps, examining each page until he could point to a picture and shout, "I've found it!"

That's one of the things I love most about babysitting: that each kid is so different, depending on his (or her) age and personality. It takes a lot of experience to know what kinds of things are fun for different kids to do. And, I must say, I have a *lot* of experience.

I love babysitting.

In fact, it's one of my favourite things to do—and I know six other girls who feel the same way. We even have a club. It's called the Babysitters Club. But I'll tell you more about that later. First of all, I'd better tell you who I am. My name is Dawn Schafer, and I live in Stoneybrook, Connecticut. I'm thirteen and I'm in the eighth grade at Stoneybrook Middle School.

I haven't always lived in Connecticut. Guess where I grew up? In California! That's right, sunny California. My life there sometimes seems like ancient history, though. I'm pretty used to living in Connecticut now. That's right, snowy Connecticut, home of the BSC. (That's shorthand for the Babysitters Club.)

The club really saved my life when I first moved here. I was pretty lonely then, and still upset about my parents' divorce. That's why we moved here, by the way—because my parents got a divorce. My dad stayed in California, but my mum and I and my younger brother Jeff (he's ten) moved to Stoneybrook, where my mum had grown up.

Mum felt comfortable here straight away, since Connecticut was so familiar to her. But it took me a lot longer to get used to living in a new place. And Jeff? Jeff never really adjusted. In fact, he disliked Connecticut so much (and missed his dad so badly on top of it) that he ended up moving back to California to live with him. I can't say I'm happy about our family being split up, but I'm glad we did what was best for Jeff.

So you probably think that it's just me and my mum living together in the big old (and I mean *old*) farmhouse we bought. But you're wrong. Something pretty exciting happened after we moved back here. Mum got together with an old high-school sweetheart of hers who still lived in Stoneybrook, and after they'd gone out together for what seemed like years, they got married! The best part is that I gained not only a stepfather (Richard Spier is his name), but a stepsister as well. And my stepsister was—and is—my best friend!

Talk about lucky.

Of course, I didn't feel all that lucky straight away. Mary Anne and I hit some rough patches before we ironed out our new relationship as stepsisters and housemates. But now a pretty happy family is living in that farmhouse: Richard and Mum, Mary Anne and me, and Tigger, Mary Anne's grey kitten.

Wow! How did I get onto the subject of Tigger? I was telling you about my sitting job at the Hobarts'. So there I was, playing find the picture with Johnny Hobart. And telling you how much I like to work out what activity is best for each kid I sit for. And I do like doing that, but I was glad I didn't have to do it for all four Hobart boys at once.

That would've been pretty tough.

Luckily for me, James and Mathew Hobart, the two middle brothers (James is eight and Mathew's six) were playing in the garden with some of the neighbourhood kids. They didn't need me to entertain them. And Ben, the oldest Hobart boy? Where was he? Well, red-haired Ben, who's a sixth-grader like my friend, fellow club-member Mallory Pike, was at the library, studying. And he wasn't alone. He was with—guess who—Mallory herself. I think something romantic may be going on between them. Isn't that exciting?

Johnny had found the shoe and had started to look for the next picture, which was of a birthday cake. I glanced at the kids playing in the side garden. James and Mathew seemed to be having a good time kicking a football around. I knew two of the kids they were playing with pretty well; Nicky Pike, who's Mallory's little brother, and Jamie Newton, who's a boy I've babysat for fairly often. The other two, Zach Wolfson and Mel Tucker, were less familiar to me, but I knew them from the neighbourhood. Zach and Mel aren't what I would call *bad* kids, but they have been known to enjoy teasing kids who are "different". Kristy once had a hard time trying to teach them not to make fun of this autistic girl, Susan.

The boys were in a circle, passing a football back and forth in some complicated pattern that I didn't quite understand. Just as I looked up to check on James and Mathew, James gave a mighty kick at the ball—and missed. It rolled behind him, out of the circle.

"What do you think you're doing, you dumb Croc?" yelled Mel.

Oh no. Not that again. I waited to see what James would do.

"I asked you not to call me that, remember?" said James to Mel. He sounded calm.

"Oh, yeah," said Mel. "Sorry. Now get the ball!"

"Yeah," said Zach. "And hurry up, Cr— I mean, James!"

I shook my head. I had thought that the kids were all getting along pretty well, but it seemed that Mel and Zach hadn't lost the habit of bullying James—and probably Mathew, too.

The Hobarts are Australian. That's why Mel calls them "Crocs". You know, for Crocodile Dundee? But the Hobart boys (understandably) hate being teased about their accents, their habits, or the strange (to us) words they sometimes use. They just want to fit in and be accepted. And for the most part, they are. Mel and Zach are the only ones who still tease them, as far as I can see.

I wonder why kids are sometimes so horrible to each other. Maybe it has more to do with the kid who's *doing* the teasing. I mean, I think kids who are bullies are probably just taking out their own problems on other kids.

Like my brother Jeff. He was never exactly a bully, but he did have a kind of behaviour problem for a while when we first moved to Stoneybrook. He'd get into fights at school, act cocky with my mum, and say really nasty things to me. At first we couldn't work out what was the matter with him. Then we began to understand that he was acting like that because he was just *so* unhappy about living in Stoneybrook.

Jeff's problem behaviour stopped as soon as he heard he was going to be allowed to move back to California. Really! He was a different person. Anyway, I keep that experience in mind when I'm dealing with kids who are, well, difficult. I try to remember that their behaviour may just be a symptom of some kind of personal problem.

I checked the side garden again, just to make sure the teasing had stopped. But it hadn't! I saw James standing there red-faced, as Zach and Mel told him again what a "dumb Croc" he was.

I was fed up with the teasing. I got to my feet and put my hands on my hips. "Zach Wolfson!" I said, trying to sound as if I was in charge, "Mel Tucker! You boys stop that right now, do you hear me?"

The two of them ducked their heads and did their best to look ashamed—for about two seconds. Then the football game started up again. I sat down, shaking my head. There really wasn't *that* much I could do about the situation.

"How's it going, Johnny?" I asked, looking back at Johnny and his magazine.

"Super!" he said, in his lovely Australian accent. "I've found all but one." He showed me the page. "I just can't find the crow." He bent over the magazine again. "I know I can find it if I try," he said.

What determination! I smiled down at Johnny. I'm a pretty determined person myself, so I can relate to him. I like doing things my own way, and I try not to let other people's opinions bother me too much. For example, I don't follow fashion trends at all. I wear my long blonde hair straight down my back most of the time (no fancy hairstyles for me, thanks) and I dress in clothes that feel comfortable to me. Most of my wardrobe is in bright colours, and it's all pretty casual stuff—loose and a bit sporty. My friends call my style "California casual".

My clothes are never too wild, but I do

get a little creative with my jewellery at times. I have two holes pierced in each ear, and I'll wear whatever combination of earrings I feel like when I get up in the morning. Two in one ear, none in the other, four non-matching earrings, whatever. Some of the kids at school probably think I'm weird, but I don't really care.

I go my own way with other things, too—food, for example. Most kids my age love junk food, but I won't go near it. Tofu and bean sprouts just *taste* better to me than crisps and chocolate. I know, I know, it's hard to believe that I actually don't like chocolate. There's almost something weird about that. But I just don't. And I don't see the point in pretending otherwise.

There is one thing I like that a lot of other kids like, too, and that's reading about ghosts. I *love* ghost stories. And guess what? There may be an actual, real ghost in my house! We have this secret passage, and I've heard some pretty weird stories about who, or what, may live in it. There have been times when I've heard noises—

"Dawn!" All of a sudden I heard my name being called. I looked up and saw Mrs Hobart struggling up the path with two huge bags of groceries. "Can you grab one of these?" she asked. "I think I'm about to drop them both."

I jumped up. "Of course," I said. I ran to

her side, took one of the bags, and followed her up the path.

"How did it go today?" she asked.

"Fine," I said. "Johnny did a great job with finding the pictures in his *Highlights* magazine, and James and Mathew have been playing in the garden all afternoon."

"They seem to be having fun," said Mrs Hobart, pausing to watch the game.

"They are," I said. "Although I did want to tell you that some teasing is still going on. Mel and Zach are calling the boys 'Crocs' once in a while."

"Oh, dear." She sighed. "I thought that had stopped. Perhaps it's time I stepped in. I'm not sure how to deal with those boys, but the name-calling just can't go on."

I followed Mrs Hobart into the kitchen and put down my bag, then turned and went back out to get another. Just as I'd pulled the last one out of the car boot, Ben and Mallory walked into the garden.

They looked so cute together, since both of them have red hair and glasses. I tried not to embarrass Mallory by staring at them.

"Here, I can take that," said Ben, taking the bag from my arms. He turned to Mal. "Do you want to come in for a snack? I'm sure Mum's laid one on," he said to her.

Oooh, I love the way he talks. And Ben is such a sweet guy. I noticed Mal blushing as she accepted his offer. Obviously she thought he was pretty sweet, too. As soon as Mrs Hobart had paid me, I jumped onto my bike and rode home as fast as I could. I couldn't wait to give Mary Anne the latest "Ben and Mallory" report.

2nd CHAPTER

Mary Anne was sitting in the living room, playing with Tigger, when I got home. She had tied a feather to an old shoelace, and she was dragging it in front of him and twitching it to make it look alive. Tigger pounced again and again, like a fierce little tiger.

"Guess who went to the library together today?" I said. I was eager to spread the news.

"Who?" asked Mary Anne, still watching Tigger.

"Ben and Mallory!" I said.

"Really?" she asked, looking up at me. "Wow. They're becoming a proper couple." She sighed. "Isn't it romantic?" She looked kind of dewy-eyed.

That's typical of Mary Anne. She's such a sensitive soul, and she cries so easily, whether she's happy or sad. I've even seen

11

her cry over those soppy telephone company adverts where the father and son are having a long distance heart-to-heart chat.

But her sensitivity is what makes Mary Anne such a good friend. She's a great listener, and she always knows the right thing to say to make you feel better if you're upset. She really pays attention to other people's feelings.

Mary Anne hasn't had the easiest life. First of all, her mum died when Mary Anne was just a baby, so it was just her and her father until Richard and my mum got married. I think Mary Anne was lonely some of the time. Also, her dad bent over backwards to fill the shoes of two parents. The result was a pretty strict set of rules for Mary Anne's behaviour. She was treated like a second-grader until only recently.

For example, Mary Anne isn't the world's wildest dresser right now, but at least she has a few cool-looking outfits. Her dad *used* to make her dress in clothes that looked far too young for her. And he used to make her wear her hair in pigtails! For the longest time Mary Anne was so shy and quiet that she just accepted his rules, even though they drove her mad.

She's still pretty shy and quiet, but Mary Anne has definitely begun to learn how to stand up for herself. With her dad, and with Logan Bruno, her off-and-on boyfriend.

Isn't it funny that Mary Anne, the shyest of all my friends, is the only one who's had a steady boyfriend? I think Logan likes her for the same reasons I do. Mary Anne and Logan have been through some tough times, but I think they'll always be close, whether they're "going out" or not.

Mary Anne and I sat quietly for a while in the living room, watching Tigger play, and I began to think about the Babysitters Club and the friends I've made since I joined it. Mary Anne was the first (she's in the club, too, of course), and she's still my *best* friend, but the others are also pretty special to me.

Kristy Thomas is Mary Anne's *other* best friend. They've known each other since day one, when they used to live next door to each other. Back then, Kristy lived with her mum, her two older brothers Charlie and Sam, and her little brother David Michael. But now Kristy's life has changed, and her family is much bigger.

Kristy's dad walked out on the family when David Michael was just a baby, and Mrs Thomas did a great job of holding the family together. But when Kristy was in the seventh grade, her mum met—and eventually married—a man called Watson Brewer. He's a millionaire. Really! And when they got married, Kristy's family moved across town to live in his mansion.

Watson was divorced, too, and he has two kids from his first marriage, Karen and Andrew. Kristy loves them, and looks forward to their visits every other weekend. She also loves Emily Michelle, the little Vietnamese girl Watson and Kristy's mum have adopted. And Kristy's very happy that Nannie, her grandmother, came to live with them to help out with Emily. It's a big, chaotic, happy household, especially when you include the pets: Shannon their puppy, Boo-Boo their old crabby cat, and Crystal Light the Second and Goldfishie, the goldfish.

Kristy seems to thrive on the constant action at her house. She loves to be right in the middle of things. I bet you're thinking that she and Mary Anne have really different personalities—and they do, but it doesn't stop them from being friends. Where Mary Anne is shy and quiet, Kristy is outspoken and bold. (Actually, she's even what some people might call a loud-mouth.)

Kristy and Mary Anne have a lot in common, too. You'd know it right away if you saw them together, since they look so much alike. They've got brown hair and brown eyes, and they're both pretty short for their age. (Kristy's the shortest girl in our class.) But while Mary Anne does have some cool clothes, as I mentioned before, Kristy doesn't have any, and she doesn't care. She's happiest dressed in jeans, a poloneck, and trainers, which is what she wears just about every day. I can't believe she doesn't get bored, but I suppose clothes aren't important to Kristy.

Clothes are *very* important to Claudia Kishi, who grew up and still lives in the street where Mary Anne and Kristy once did. She is just about the wildest dresser I've ever seen. You can't imagine some of the crazy outfits she comes up with. But she always looks great.

Of course, Claudia would look great even if she were dressed in a brown paper bag. She's gorgeous. She's Japanese-American, and she has these beautiful dark brown almond-shaped eyes and long black silky hair. Sometimes I wish I looked as exotic as Claudia.

Claudia's incredibly creative and talented. She can paint, draw, and make sculptures. She even makes her own jewellery. There's nothing she loves as much as art. She's so clever, too. If she'd put as much energy into her schoolwork as she does her art classes, she'd be getting straight "A"s. But I suppose she thinks that one "A" student per family is enough, and her older sister Janine the Genius takes care of things in that department.

Apart from art, Claudia's passions include junk food and reading Nancy Drew mysteries. Her parents don't approve of either habit, so Claudia has got used to hiding chocolate, crisps, and books all over her room. You can't pick up a pillow without finding a Mars Bar underneath it. I used to try to lecture Claudia about how bad junk food is, but I've given up trying to convince her. Claud will never give up her junk food!

Claud's best friend is Stacey McGill. They share a love for wild clothes and accessories, but Stacey has to stay away from the junk food. She's a diabetic, which means her body doesn't do a good job of dealing with sugar. She has to be very, very careful about what she eats. She also has to give herself injections of this stuff called insulin, which her body doesn't produce properly.

Can you imagine giving yourself injections every *day*? I can't. But Stacey doesn't make a big deal about it. She just does it because she knows she has to. If she doesn't, she could get really ill. In fact, not too long ago she ended up in hospital. Her blood sugar had got totally out of control.

Stacey grew up in New York City, and she's just as sophisticated as you can imagine. Not only is she a great dresser, but she also does really interesting things with her blonde hair. Sometimes she gets it permed, so it's all curly and wild. She's allowed to wear make-up, and she knows how to apply it so that she looks good—

unlike some of the other girls at school, who look as if they should be on a stage under bright lights!

Stacey's parents are divorced, and her dad lives in New York. Stacey could have lived with him, but she decided she'd be happier living in Stoneybrook with her mum. Being a divorced kid is never easy (believe me, I know), but Stacey's learning to deal with her situation. She visits her father as often as she can.

Kristy and Mary Anne and Stacey and Claud are all thirteen and in the eighth grade, like me. But the two other members of our club are a bit younger. They are Mallory Pike (possible future girlfriend of Ben Hobart) and Jessi Ramsey. They're both eleven and in the sixth grade.

Mal is pretty grown up for her age. I think that's because she's the eldest child in a really big family. She's got *seven* brothers and sisters. I love hearing her reel off their names in order of their ages, oldest to youngest. It sounds like this: "Adam-ByronJordanVanessaNickyMargoClaire!" Actually, Adam, Byron and Jordan are the same age (ten). They're triplets!

Remember how I said Kristy's house could be chaotic? Well, it's nothing compared to the Pikes'. Mal's house is like a three-ring circus. In fact, if all the kids are at home, *two* BSC members are needed for a sitting job. (One of them is usually Mal.)

Mallory's main problem is that, although her parents consider her very mature and have given her a lot of responsibility in the family, they won't "let her grow up." I remember feeling the same way. When I was eleven what I wanted most was to be thirteen, or at least to be treated like I was thirteen. I wanted to wear make-up and get my ears pierced, and I wanted to wear cool clothes.

But the Pikes, like many parents, aren't ready for their little girl to be a teenager. They did finally relent and let Mal get her ears pierced (just one hole in each ear), but she's still not allowed to dress too wildly. And her parents aren't ready to let her get contact lenses instead of glasses. She'll have to wait a while for that. I think Mal's glasses wouldn't bother her so much if it weren't for the fact that she *also* has to wear a brace.

Mal loves reading—especially horse stories—and writing, and she's also a pretty good artist. One day she'd like to write and illustrate children's books.

Jessi Ramsey is Mal's best friend. She also loves to read horse stories, and wishes her parents would let her grow up. Beyond that, Jessi and Mal are pretty different. For one thing, Jessi's black and Mal's white. There aren't too many black families in Stoneybrook, and when the Ramseys first moved here they weren't made to feel all that welcome. But now people have got to know them, so things are better.

I don't see how anyone could be mean to Jessi's family. They're great! Jessi's got a little sister called Becca, and a baby brother called Squirt. He's gorgeous.

Jessi's main passion is ballet. She's a serious pupil who loves to dance. Jessi's really talented—I've seen her perform the lead role in more than one of her school's productions. She's considering a career as a ballerina, and I think she's got what it takes.

It must be obvious to you by now that I've got a special group of friends. I feel really lucky to know them all.

"Don't you, Dawn?"

Mary Anne was asking me something. I blinked and looked over at her. "What?" I replied. I'd been lost in thought.

"Don't you think Tigger is the sweetest cat in the world?" she asked. He was sitting on her lap, purring as she scratched behind his ears.

"Definitely," I said. "No question about it." I smiled at him. "And I'm certainly glad he lets me be best friends with his owner."

3rd CHAPTER

"Okay, Mal, tell all," said Claud.

Wow. Word had travelled fast. My friends and I had gathered in Claud's room for a BSC meeting. Only a few days had passed since that afternoon at the Hobarts', but every single member of the club already knew about Ben and Mallory going to the library together.

Mallory blushed. "What?" she asked. "Tell all *what*? Nothing happened."

"'Nothing' meaning *nothing*?" asked Claud, her eyes shining as she tried to hide a grin. "Or 'nothing' meaning 'I just don't want to tell you'?"

"C'mon, Claud, let her be," said Kristy. "It's time to get down to business, anyway. I hereby call this meeting to order." Kristy leaned back in the director's chair and pushed up the visor she was wearing. The room was quiet for a few seconds. Then

Kristy took the pencil from behind her ear and started to tap it on the arm of her chair. "So, any club business?" she asked. "If not, maybe Mallory has some news to share with us." She grinned.

"I thought you told me to lay off!" said Claud. "I *knew* you were just as curious as anyone else."

Kristy probably *was* curious about what had happened between Ben and Mallory. She likes to hear about that kind of stuff just as much as we all do, even though she's not terribly interested in boys yet herself. Actually, now that I think of it, she *is* kind of interested in one boy, this guy named Bart who lives in her neighbourhood.

But Kristy doesn't usually let gossip get in the way of a professionally run Baby-sitters Club meeting. She's chairman of our club, and she takes her job seriously. She takes the whole club pretty seriously, in fact, and that's one of the reasons the club works so well. We run it like a business, a business our clients know they can depend on.

I should explain that the original idea for the club was Kristy's. That's why she's chairman. She's had lots of great ideas, but I'd have to say that the idea for the club was her best ever.

Here's how it happened: Back in the seventh grade, Kristy and her brothers were responsible for looking after David Michael whenever Mrs Thomas was at work or wanted to go out. That was fine with them—especially with Kristy, who's always loved babysitting. But there were times when Sam had a meeting, and Charlie had a date, and Kristy had plans, too. Then Mrs Thomas would have to start making phone calls, looking for a sitter.

Anyway, that's exactly what had happened one afternoon. Kristy's mum was dialling frantically, phoning everyone she knew. Every sitter she tried was busy, or ill, or had other plans. Mrs Thomas was getting discouraged. But Kristy? Kristy was getting excited because she'd had a *great* idea.

What if her mum could have called *one* number that would have put her in touch with a whole group of experienced sitters? Someone would certainly be available.

You know, I've never found out whether Mrs Thomas found a sitter that afternoon. But in the long run, it doesn't matter. What matters is that the Babysitters Club was born. Kristy talked to Mary Anne and Claudia, and they loved the idea straightaway. Claud suggested that her new friend Stacey could join too. Then when I moved to Stoneybrook I became part of the club as well. Jessi and Mal joined later on, and now we think the size of the club is perfect.

Speaking of Jessi and Mal, at that moment during the club meeting, the two of them had got a terrible case of the giggles. They were rolling around on the floor, crashing into furniture and people, and laughing so hard they couldn't stop. Claud picked up her feet as they rolled near where she sat on her bed. "Hey, you two, you'd better settle down!" she said, glancing at Kristy. Kristy likes to keep our meetings business-like, as I've said. Giggles are not business-like.

Jessi sat up straight and tried to stifle her laughter. So did Mal. But by then, the rest of us were giggling, too. I suppose it was contagious.

"What are we laughing at?" asked Stacey.

"I don't know," I said. "But I bet it's got something to do with Ben."

Jessi nodded through her giggles. She was holding her stomach. "Ben's friend Jim told me that Ben thinks Mal is a 'bonzer sheila'."

"A *what*?" asked Claud.

"Is that *good*?" I asked at the same time.

"It's good," said Jessi. "It means that she's a great girl. And that he likes her."

Mallory punched Jessi in the arm. "Shhh!" she said, blushing.

"All I said was that—" But Jessi didn't

get a chance to finish her sentence, as just then the phone rang.

I suppose I forgot to tell you that that's the whole point of these meetings. Basically, we're waiting for the phone to ring. Clients know that if they want to arrange jobs, they can call us between five-thirty and six on Mondays, Wednesdays, and Fridays. During those times, the line is only open to our clients, because it's Claud's private line. That's right—Claud has not only her own phone, but her own line. That's why we meet in her room. And that's why she's vice-chairman of the club.

You may be wondering how our clients know our phone number. Well, a lot of them get it from friends, from other parents who have used our service and liked it. That's called "word of mouth advertising". But even though we get a lot of business that way, sometimes we advertise normally, too. We place an ad in the local paper, or, more often, we pass out leaflets that include all the information a client would need. The club has plenty of business—all the business it can handle, as a matter of fact.

So, anyway, the phone had just rung, and we'd all made a grab for it. But Kristy had grabbed quickest. "Hello?" she said. "Babysitters Club."

We quietened down so we could listen.

It's fun to try and guess, from Kristy's side of the conversation, who's calling. "Tuesday at three?" she asked. "I'm sure we can have somebody there. How long will you need a sitter for?"

She paused. There was still no way for the rest of us to know whom she was talking to. "That's fine," she said, after a moment. "As long as Jamie knows we'll be giving him dinner."

Jamie. That meant Mrs Newton was calling, looking for a sitter for Jamie, who's four, and for his baby sister Lucy. We all love sitting for the Newtons, since Jamie's a great kid and we're mad about babies.

"Okay, then," Kristy was saying. "I'll call you back." She hung up and turned to Mary Anne. "Mary Anne," she said. "Mrs Newton needs somebody on Tuesday starting at three o'clock and going straight through 'til nine. Who's available?"

Mary Anne checked the record book. She's our club secretary, and she does an awesome job of keeping track of our schedules. It's all there in that book: Jessi's dance lessons, Kristy's softball games, Claud's art classes . . . not to mention our sitting jobs, plus information (such as addresses and phone numbers) about our clients.

"Well, Jessi and Mal are out since it's a weeknight," Mary Anne said straight away.

25

Jessi made a face. She and Mal aren't allowed to sit on weeknights—except for their own brothers and sisters—which is why they are what we call "junior officers". They do a lot of work during afternoons and weekends, though, which is a big help because it frees the rest of us up for evening jobs.

"And Kristy, you have a job already, at the Perkinses," Mary Anne went on. "Claud has an art lesson that day, which means that the only sitters available are Dawn and Stacey. And me, of course."

"One of you can take it," said Stacey. "I've got plenty of other jobs."

Mary Anne looked at me. "Want to flip a coin?" she asked.

"No, that's okay," I said. "You take it. I know you always have a great time sitting for Jamie and Lucy. I'm going to be busy anyway, because of that humongous English project I have to do."

So it was settled. Kristy phoned Mrs Newton back and told her that Mary Anne would be there. And that's how the system works! Pretty cool, right?

By this time next week, we'd all know just how the job at the Newtons had gone, too, because Mary Anne would have written it up in the club notebook. That's not the same as the record book. It's more like a diary in which we each tell the others about our sitting jobs and about any special client information we may want to share. The notebook was Kristy's idea, and while none of us *loves* writing up our jobs, we have to admit that the information is useful.

Let's see. I've told you that Kristy is the chairman and Claud is the vice-chairman. I've told you that Mary Anne is the secretary and that Jessi and Mal are junior officers. What about Stacey and me?

Well, Stacey's the treasurer. She keeps track of how much money each member has earned. She also collects subs once a week (on Mondays) and she's in charge of the treasury. That means that if we want to have a pizza party or some other special club event, we need to check with Stacey to make sure we have enough money.

We also use subs for more serious things than pizza, by the way. We use some of it to pay Kristy's brother for chauffeuring her to meetings three times a week, since she lives too far away to walk. And we use some of it to keep our Kid-Kits full of goodies.

What are Kid-Kits? They're another of Kristy's great ideas. They're boxes that we've decorated to look really cool and have then filled with toys and books and games that kids love. Not all of the stuff in our Kid-Kits is new, but it's all new to the kids we sit for, so they love to see the Kid-Kits.

I bet you think I've forgotten to tell you

27

what *my* job is. Well, you're wrong. I'll tell you now. I'm the alternate officer, which means I know how to do everybody else's job, and I can take over if and when they can't make a meeting. For example, I was the treasurer for a while when Stacey's family temporarily moved back to New York City. (I didn't mind doing her job, but I didn't *love* it. I was happy to give it back to her when she moved back to Stoneybrook.)

There are two other people who belong to our club, even though they don't attend meetings. They are our associate members, Shannon Kilbourne and Logan Bruno (that's right, Mary Anne's boyfriend). They're available to step in whenever we get more business than we can handle, and that's happened more than once!

"Hey, Jessi," said Claudia, after we'd taken some more calls. "*What* was it that Ben called Mallory?"

"A bonzer sheila," said Jessi, giggling again. "Bonzer means terrific, and sheila means—like, *girl*. It comes from the name they call female ka—kan—" All of a sudden Jessi was laughing so hard that she couldn't get the word out.

"What are you trying to tell us?" asked Claud. "That sheila is the word for a female *kangaroo*?" She burst out laughing. "I don't believe it. Ben called Mal a kangaroo, and he meant it as a compliment?"

By then we were all laughing, including Mal, who had gone bright red as soon as the subject of Ben had come up again. By that time it was six o'clock, and in order to adjourn the meeting, Kristy had to shout over our giggles. Another "business-like" club meeting had come to an end.

4th CHAPTER

" 'Bye, Dawn," said Kristy. "Have a great time!" She was heading out of the door with her mother. I had come to sit for her little brothers and sisters while Kristy and Mrs Brewer went shopping.

"'Bye, Kristy!" yelled Karen. "Don't forget you promised to bring me a present!"

"I won't," said Kristy, smiling.

"Do I get a present, too?" yelled David Michael. "I want one, too!"

"Me, too!" shouted Andrew.

"Me me me!" yelled Emily Michelle. She had no idea of what was going on, but she wanted to get in on whatever it was.

"You'll all get something," said Kristy. "But remember, don't expect anything major. I'm not coming home with any Nintendo games or Barbie Playhouses."

The kids nodded. "Last time she brought me the most prettiest bow for my hair,"

30

Karen told me, her eyes shining. "Kristy's the best big sister in the world."

I nodded. "She thinks you're a pretty great *little* sister, too," I said. I waved at Kristy as her mum's car pulled out of the drive. "Have fun!" I yelled. Kristy made a face. Shopping is not one of her favourite activities. To be honest, I wouldn't be too excited either, if I were her. All she was going to get was a new pair of jeans and maybe a new poloneck. When you dress like Kristy, shopping isn't exactly a thrilling adventure.

"Okay, gang," I said, herding the four kids into the kitchen. "You're allowed to have a snack, so let's see what there is." I checked the cupboards as Karen, David Michael, and Andrew jostled each other for seats at the table. Emily Michelle climbed into her high chair and gave a happy screech when she found a spoon there that she could play with.

"How about some Cheddars?" I asked, showing them the box.

"Yea!" yelled Karen, Andrew, and David Michael. Emily Michelle waved her spoon in the air.

I brought the box to the table and offered it to Karen. "Take a few," I said, "and then we'll pass it round."

She gave me a funny look. "That's not how you eat crackers," she said.

"Oh, no?" I asked, raising my eyebrows. "It's how *I* eat crackers."

"No," she said. "Usually we each get our own little bowl. Then we each count how many crackers we have and make sure we all have the same amount. Then we have a contest to see who can eat them the slowest."

"I see," I said. What a production! Kids love to make a big deal out of the simplest things. But it was fine with me. I divided their crackers into four bowls and delivered them to the table.

They counted their crackers carefully (Karen counted Emily Michelle's for her) and then swapped back and forth until they all had the same number. They started on their "slow eating" contest, but then David Michael decided to start a different contest.

"How many can you fit in your mouth at one time?" he asked Karen. He began stuffing crackers into his mouth, counting as he went. "One, two, three, fow, wive, thix, thev—"

"David Michael!" I said. "Stop!" I was afraid he was going to choke. His cheeks looked like a chipmunk's. "That's not a good idea for a contest. Why don't you go back to eating slowly, and maybe you can all tell me what's new with you."

"Goldfishie and Crystal Light the Second are getting married!" exclaimed Karen. "That's what's new."

"Getting married?" I asked. I've told you about Goldfishie and Crystal Light. They're fish. Plain little goldfish that swim around and around all day. But Karen loves them—and she has an active imagination.

"Goldfishie asked Crystal Light to marry him, and soon they're going to have a fishy wedding," said Karen. "You can be invited if you want."

I tried to imagine a fishy wedding. Would Crystal Light wear a tiny white veil? Would she carry a bouquet of seaweed in her fin? I almost laughed aloud, but I caught myself in time. Karen might be hurt if I acted as if there was anything funny about two fish getting married.

I noticed that everyone had finished with their crackers, except Emily Michelle who was busy trying to stick them into her ears. "Let's go into the TV room," I said, "and you can tell me more about the wedding."

We trooped into the TV room, and I sat on the sofa with Emily Michelle on my lap. Karen sat by my feet and starting chattering on about Crystal Light the Second. Andrew found his favourite toy aeroplane and started to run around the room with it, making engine noises. We were all settled in. I gave a little yawn while I listened to Karen talk. I was sleepy from staying up late watching a film the night before. I was glad I didn't have to be "super-sitter" that

33

afternoon. These kids were pretty good at entertaining themselves.

Then I noticed something. Only three kids were in the room with me. Where was David Michael?

"Dawn!" I heard my name called from the doorway. I looked up and there was David Michael. With a camera in his hand. "Smile!" he said as the flash went off.

"What are you doing?" I asked.

He pulled the picture out of the camera and held it up to his face, watching it as it developed. "Shhh," he said. "Just a minute. I want to make sure this came out okay."

I shook my head. What was he up to? After a moment, he showed the picture to me. "I think you look pretty in this," he said.

I took a look. Pretty? I looked as if I'd just seen a ghost. That flash had surprised me. Karen jumped up to look over my shoulder. "Beautiful," she said.

"It'll look great in the newspaper," said David Michael. "That is, if you win."

"Newspaper?" I asked. "Win *what*? What's going on here, anyway?"

"It's a contest," said David Michael. "You know how the supermarket has those ads in the paper that show the 'check-out girl of the week'?"

I nodded.

"Well, some kids at school decided we

should have a contest for 'Sitter of the Month'. If you win, we'll send your photo in to the paper." He looked at me with an expectant smile.

"Wow," I said. "That's a great idea. How do you *choose* the Sitter of the Month?"

"We vote," he said. "Mrs Newton—Jamie's mum?—is helping us run the elections. Whichever sitter is the most fun and the nicest and the best babysitter will win."

Hmmm . . . nicest? Well, I'd been pretty nice so far. I'd given the kids a snack and I'd been listening to Karen's stories. Best sitter? I'd certainly been responsible. Most fun? Well, I could use some improvement there. Because I was feeling sleepy, I hadn't exactly been a barrel of laughs that day.

I sat up straight and smiled. "Sounds like a great contest," I said. "Now, what are we doing just sitting around? Let's get busy! How about a game of Let's All Come In!"

"Yea!" said Karen, throwing her hands in the air. Let's All Come In is her favourite game, maybe because she's the one who made it up. It's a "let's pretend" game that takes place in a lobby of a big, fancy hotel. One person plays the receptionist, and their job is to greet the guests and help them sign in. The other players dress up as different characters and take turns making "entrances".

Karen was dancing around the room with

35

Emily Michelle. "Let's All Come In!" she sang. Emily Michelle giggled and shrieked as Karen spun her round. Andrew laughed as he watched them.

"Karen," he shouted. "I don't want to be a dog, okay?" Andrew used to get the worst parts in Let's All Come In, just because he was the youngest. He'd get angry when Karen would make him be some rich lady's dog.

"Okay, Andrew," Karen yelled back. "Emily can be the dog." Emily nodded and laughed.

I was glad my idea had caused so much excitement. Obviously, one of the things a Sitter of the Month should be good at is coming up with fun activities. Then I noticed something. Not *all* of my charges were excited about playing Let's All Come In. In fact, one of them looked downright unhappy about it. David Michael was standing in the doorway with his arms folded across his chest and a sour look on his face.

"I hate that stupid game. It's for babies," he said.

"No it's not," I said. "*I'm* going to play it, and I'm thirteen years old. I'm no baby."

"Well, it's stupid and boring," he said. "We always have the same characters. Mrs Noswimple. Mrs Mysterious. Bo-ring."

I thought fast. "How about if we make up some new characters?" I asked. "Come here, David Michael. Let's plan." I waved him over and started to whisper in his ear.

"Ready to start?" asked Karen. She hopped across the room excitedly. "I'll go upstairs and find an outfit. David Michael, you be the receptionist." Karen can be a little bossy.

"Just a minute, Karen," I said. "David Michael and I have something to say. We think it's *your* turn to be the receptionist."

Karen's eyes widened. "My turn?" she asked. "But—"

"No buts," I said. "David Michael is only going to play if you'll be the receptionist."

Karen shrugged. "Well, okay, I suppose so," she said. She ran into the living room and grabbed an exercise book and a pencil from Watson's desk and took a pretty china bell from a shelf above the fireplace. Then she settled herself behind the coffee table and began to arrange her check-in desk.

David Michael, Andrew, and I ran to the playroom and raided the dressing-up chest. Our first guest was easy, since David Michael was wearing jeans and a white T-shirt. I rolled up the sleeves of his shirt so that he looked tough, and stuck a red bandana in his back pocket. Then we all went downstairs.

David Michael walked up to the desk and rang the bell.

"Yes?" asked Karen. "May I help you?"

"I'm Bruce Stringbean," said David Michael, giggling. "I'm a big rock and roll star and I need a room for me and my manager and all my friends."

Karen cracked up. "Bruce Stringbean?" she said. "Okay, Mr Stringbean, will you please sign here."

The next guest David Michael and I created was Darryl Blueberry, the baseball star. Then I dressed as Ladonna, the beautiful singer. Karen could not stop laughing. Neither could David Michael. We played for the rest of the afternoon, and when I left that day, David Michael told me I was his favourite sitter. I went home happy, certain I was well on my way to being voted the first Sitter of the Month.

5th
CHAPTER

"Bruce *String*bean?" asked Jessi. "How did you ever come up with that one?" She was laughing, and so was everybody else in Claud's room. It was Monday afternoon and we were having a club meeting, but we hadn't done much business yet.

I was sitting on the bed next to Mary Anne. Claudia was also on the bed. She was leaning against the wall, sucking on an orange Ice Pop. Jessi and Mal were sitting on the floor, as usual. They were passing a bag of crisps back and forth. Stacey was sitting in Claud's desk chair, making tiny plaits in her hair.

"You're going to have to do the back for me, Claud," she said. "I can't reach there."

"No probs," said Claud. "Just come over here whenever you're ready."

"You'd better not get any Ice Pop juice on me," Stacey joked.

"I'll wash my hands," said Claud.

"Is this what you lot call club business?" asked Kristy. She was sitting in the director's chair, looking slightly peeved. It had been a few minutes since she'd brought the meeting to order, but so far we hadn't talked about anything serious.

We'd been too busy talking about Bruce Stringbean.

"*Well*?" asked Kristy, when none of us answered.

After a moment, Stacey spoke up. "Well, it *is* Monday," she said. "And you all know what that means."

We groaned. Time to pay subs.

Stacey pulled out the manila envelope that she keeps our treasury in and passed it to Jessi. "Pay up!" she said, a big smile on her face. Stacey just *loves* collecting our money. And, needless to say, we *hate* giving it up. She watched closely as each of us put our subs into the envelope. Then, when it came back to her, she counted the money (she can do that in about three seconds— Stacey's such a maths whiz) and heaved a big, satisfied sigh. "Looking good!" she said.

The phone rang just then, and Stacey, Claud, and Kristy all dived for it. Stacey grabbed it first. "Hello? Babysitters Club," she said. She paused. "Oh, hi, Mrs Korman. A week from Friday? Oh, I'm sure we can have someone there. We'll call you right back, okay?" She hung up.

Mary Anne was already checking the notebook. "Looks as if it's you or me, Kristy," she said. "Why don't you take it, since the Kormans live in your neighbourhood?"

"Fine with me," said Kristy. "I like Bill and Melody a lot. They're good kids. And Skylar is the cutest baby." She reached for the phone and called Mrs Korman back to arrange the details of the job. When she had finished with the call, she looked around the room at us and said, "Okay, everybody. Let's talk about this Sitter of the Month thing."

I'd been wondering when somebody was going to bring it up. I knew that everybody knew about it—word had spread fast—but so far we hadn't talked about it.

The room was quiet for a minute or so. Then Mary Anne spoke up. "I think it's really sweet that the kids want to do this," she said. "I mean, don't you think it's pretty nice?"

"I think it would be a real honour to win," said Jessi. "It would mean that the kids really like you. I'd *love* to be Sitter of the Month."

"So would I," said Mallory quietly.

"I think we'd all like to win," said Kristy. "It would mean a lot to me to be the first one chosen as Sitter of the Month. I just wish I knew more about how we're going to be judged."

"You mean, like are they going to pick the one who they think lets them get away with the most, or the one who's nicest, or maybe the one who makes the best snacks?" I asked. "In order to win, you really need to know what makes kids like certain baby-sitters more than others."

"David Michael and Karen certainly liked *you* a lot the other day," said Kristy. She sounded a bit annoyed. "David Michael kept telling me that that was the 'funnest' game of Let's All Come In that he'd ever played."

I blushed. I was hoping that Kristy hadn't guessed that the *reason* the game was so fun was because I was trying so hard to be Sitter of the Month material. "It *was* fun," I said. "I think we had got a little bit tired of the same old characters."

"Right," said Kristy. "So 'super-sitter' spiced up the game."

Uh oh. Kristy was pretty annoyed.

"Hey, you two," said Mary Anne. "What's going on? We're not going to get all competitive about this, are we?" She looked upset. "I mean, of course we all want to win the contest, but let's not let it get out of hand."

"Mary Anne's right," said Stacey. "We've got to stick together. Competing with each other never gets us anywhere."

"It certainly doesn't," said Jessi. "Remember the science fair? I got so carried away trying to help Jackie Rodowsky to win that I forgot that *learning* was the point of the fair, not winning."

"What was his project again?" asked Claud. "A tornado or something?"

"A *volcano*," said Jessi. "It was a volcano that erupted lava and ash all over the place—including all over the judges of the science fair!"

"It was pretty cool," said Mallory. "Jackie did a good job on that volcano."

"Not really," said Jessi, looking shamefaced. "*I* did the good job. I wanted him to win so badly that I ended up doing most of the work for him. I didn't *mean* to cheat. I just got caught up in the competition."

"That's exactly my point," said Stacey. "When we start competing with each other, we forget everything. Good sportsmanship, fair play—everything goes out of the window and all we can think about is *winning*."

"But I like to win," said Kristy quietly.

"We all do," said Mary Anne. "But it's more important for us to stick together and support each other."

"Right," said Claud. "I mean, remember the Little Miss Stoneybrook contest?"

Oh, no. I was hoping nobody would bring

that up. What a mess! What had happened was that Claudia, Kristy, Mary Anne, and I each decided to help some of the girls we sit for to enter a talent and beauty contest.

None of the little girls was being competitive. It was us, the supposedly mature babysitters, who got carried away. We kept secrets from each other, we spied on each other, we played dirty tricks. Each of us was determined that "our" girl would win the title of Little Miss Stoneybrook.

"That was the worst," said Claudia. "We tried to make those girls into perfect robots, into the kind of girls we thought the judges would like."

In the end, *none* of the girls we'd coached won the first prize (although one of them *was* the first runner-up). The winner was this girl named Sabrina Bouvier, who was what Claudia called a "pageant-head". She knew *exactly* what the judges were looking for (including tons of make-up) and gave it to them. Our girls were disappointed, but we were relieved that the pageant was over.

"Well, let's just keep the pageant and the science fair in mind when we're thinking about this contest," said Stacey.

"Right," said Mary Anne. "No back-biting."

"Yeah," said Mallory. "Let's not get too competitive."

"I agree," said Jessi. "No campaigning."

I blushed. Had I been "campaigning" with David Michael the other day? I had certainly done my best to show him that I was a fun, exciting, and creative sitter. And there wasn't anything wrong with being those things. But would I have been quite as creative with the Let's All Come In game if I hadn't heard about the Sitter of the Month contest?

The phone rang again, and Kristy answered it. Mrs Rodowsky was calling, looking for a sitter for Jackie, Archie, and Shea. I happened to be the only one free, so I got the job. I called Mrs Rodowsky back to let her know I'd be there, and as soon as I'd hung up I caught myself thinking about the best way to impress the Rodowsky boys. They'd be voting, too!

Whoops. I was getting competitive again. I was going to have to watch that.

The phone rang a few more times, and by the time the meeting had ended we were booked up for the week. Everybody was being kind of quiet, and I wondered whether we were thinking about the same thing: the contest.

Mary Anne and I cycled home after the meeting. Usually we talk and laugh a lot as we pedal along, but that night we didn't say much. I looked at her out of the corner of my eye as she cycled next to me.

45

"Mary Anne," I said. "You'd like to be Sitter of the Month, wouldn't you?"

She nodded shyly. "I would," she said. "But only if I can win it fairly. I *hate* it when we start to compete."

I nodded in agreement. "I do, too," I said. "But I'm sure we can avoid that, since we've talked it over." I smiled at her. "It'll be a fair contest," I assured her. But you know what? I was already beginning to wonder if that was true.

6th CHAPTER

"No, not like that. Like *this*!" Jenny said. She gave me a nasty look. "You don't know how to do it right."

"I do too!" I said, feeling stupid for getting into a "do-too—do-not" argument with a four-year-old. But I *did* know how to put a nappy on a baby. Only Jenny thought that in this case, since the baby happened to be her sister, she knew better.

"Andrea doesn't like the pins so tight," she said, tugging at them in order to loosen them. Andrea gave a little shriek as Jenny pulled at her nappy. "See? She's crying because they're too tight," she said.

"She's *crying* because you—oh, never mind," I said. I was sitting at the Prezziosos', and the last thing I wanted was to get into a wrangle with Jenny. Why was it the last thing? Well, for two reasons. Reason A: Jenny can be a bit of a problem sometimes. I mean, well, she can be a real brat. There, I've said it. I like Jenny, I really do. But I think she's a little spoiled. She's used to getting her own way.

Now where was I? Oh, right. B. Well, B is, of course, that the Sitter of the Month would not be getting into arguments with her charge. She'd be calm and sweet and understanding. I let Jenny finish "fixing" Andrea's nappy. Then I smiled gently at Jenny as I pulled a pair of pyjamas out of Andrea's chest of drawers.

"Not *those* pyjamas," said Jenny. "Andrea hates those. She likes the pink ones best." She pulled a pink pair from the drawer.

I clenched my teeth. "Those are very pretty, Jenny," I said. "But I think they're a bit too warm for tonight. We don't want Andrea to get overheated." A good sitter makes careful choices about what her charges should be wearing.

"Hmph," said Jenny. "Okay. But *I'm* going to put them on her." She grabbed the pyjamas from my hand (after throwing the pink ones to the floor) and started to shove Andrea's arms into the leg holes.

I bent to pick up the pink pyjamas. (A good sitter doesn't leave a mess.) "Okay, Jenny," I said, *very* patiently, "good job. Only I think her arms are supposed to go in *here*." I showed her how to get Andrea's squirmy little arms into the sleeves of her pyjamas.

"I knew that," Jenny said, scowling. "Now we need to rock her," she added. "It helps her go to sleep."

"I know," I said. I picked up Andrea, walked to the rocking chair with her, and sat down.

"You've forgotten her blanket!" said Jenny. "She likes to have her blanket while she's being rocked."

I rolled my eyes. "Do you want to be a big helper and bring it to me?" I asked.

"No," she said. "I want to rock Andrea. I know how to do it right. *You* get the blanket." She climbed onto the rocker next to me and waited for me to put the baby into her lap. Andrea, who looked tired and grumpy, started to cry.

"Okay, Jenny, that's it," I said. I had been trying to be patient with Jenny, but she was driving me mad. She seemed to think she knew best for Andrea, and she wasn't giving me a chance to show off what a good sitter I can be. I lifted Jenny out of the rocking chair and stood her on the floor. "I want you to go downstairs and wait for me there while I put Andrea down for the night."

"I won't," said Jenny, putting her hands on her hips.

"Oh, yes you will," I said firmly. I wasn't

about to get into another argument with her. "Go on, now."

Jenny pouted. "Can I at least kiss Andrea goodnight?" she asked.

"Of course," I said. "It's nice that you love your baby sister so much." I watched as Jenny kissed Andrea on the forehead, and then I nodded to her. "Okay, go on. I'll be down in a minute."

Jenny flounced out of the door. I turned my attention to Andrea, who looked as if she were almost ready to fall asleep. I rocked her and started to sing. "Hush, little baby—"

Just then the phone rang. Drat. "Jenny," I called as quietly as I could. She didn't answer. The phone kept ringing. "Jenny," I called a little louder. "Please answer the phone!"

Finally the ringing stopped. But Jenny didn't yell up the stairs to tell me who had called. I shrugged. Maybe the person had hung up before Jenny had reached the phone.

I continued to rock Andrea and sing to her. Her eyelids flickered, and then fell shut. After I'd laid her in her cot and tucked her in, I went downstairs. Jenny was in the living room, drawing with crayons. "Nice picture," I said, looking at her artwork. She reached for a yellow crayon, and didn't answer. "Who was on the phone?" I asked.

"Mr Nobody," said Jenny, without looking up.

"What do you mean, Mr Nobody?" I asked.

"Nobody was there when I said hello," answered Jenny.

"Are you sure?"

"Yes," said Jenny. "Mr Nobody. I'm sure."

I didn't know what to think. Was Jenny telling the truth, or was she still feeling angry because I'd sent her out of Andrea's room? I thought about asking her again, but I didn't want to make her even crosser. I decided to drop the subject.

"Want to play Candy Land?" I asked Jenny. I happen to know that Candy Land is Jenny's favourite game. I personally can't stand it because it's so, so boring, but the Sitter of the Month has to do what her charges like to do.

"Nope," said Jenny, reaching for a blue crayon.

"You don't?" I asked, surprised.

"No, I'm drawing," she said.

"Can I draw, too?" I asked. If you can't beat 'em, join 'em, I decided. (I'd been planning to let her win at Candy Land, anyway.)

"No," she said. "I need all my crayons."

"Oh." All of a sudden I felt that I was *bothering* Jenny. She seemed to want to be left alone. I decided to do whatever would make her happiest, so we spent the next half hour sitting quietly in the living room. Jenny kept on drawing, and I looked at an incredibly boring magazine about computers.

After a while I checked my watch. "Oops, Jenny," I said. "It's past your bedtime. Let's get you ready for bed."

Luckily Jenny didn't put up a fight, and she was washed and in her pyjamas in no time. I read her a story (*The Sleepy Little Rabbit*) and gave her a kiss. "Goodnight, Jenny," I said.

" 'Night," she murmured. She was already half asleep. I tiptoed out of her room and down the stairs.

My homework was waiting for me on the kitchen table. I made a face. I wasn't exactly in the mood to work on fractions and decimals. I decided to write a letter to Jeff instead. I owed him one.

"Dear Jeff," I wrote on a piece of paper torn out of my English notebook. "How are you? How's good old California? I miss you."

What a boring start. I crumpled up the paper and decided to try again.

"Dearest Little Bro," I wrote. "What's up? What's fresh? Everything's cool back here in Stoneybrook. What's happening out there in sunny Cal?"

That was better.

I told Jeff the latest news about the neighbourhood and about our mother. "Mum actually cleaned out the fridge the other day," I wrote. (Our mum isn't the world's best housekeeper.) "Guess what she found? That toy plane you lost when you were visiting. I'll send it soon."

I also told Jeff about the Sitter of the Month contest, but I tried not to make a big deal out of it. I didn't want to sound too desperate to win it.

And then, just as I was adding a funny P.S., the doorbell rang. I have to tell you I almost jumped out of my seat. I checked my watch. Could it be the Prezziosos, home early? Maybe they'd forgotten their key. I ran to the front door, my heart beating fast, and peered through the window.

Nobody was there.

My heart skipped a beat. First the phone rang and, according to Jenny, nobody was there when she picked it up. Next the doorbell rang, and nobody was *there*, either. What was going on?

I looked out the window again, just to be sure. Then I unlocked the door and opened it a crack, keeping the chain on, and I saw something white on the front step. An envelope!

I unlatched the chain and opened the door just wide enough to bend down and grab the envelope. Then I stepped back inside and locked the door behind me.

I brought the envelope to the kitchen table and looked at it for a minute. I had a creepy feeling about that little white packet. Finally, I opened it and pulled out a letter.

Wow! Talk about creepy. Did you ever see those letters that kidnappers send, you know, in the films? They're made out of little letters cut out of magazines and newspapers. Criminals do that so nobody can trace their writing, I suppose.

Well that's what this letter looked like. Here's what it said:

You'd better watch out, you'd better not shout! I'm going to get you.

And it was signed, *Mr X*.

I shuddered. Who could have left this awful thing on the doorstep? Was it Jenny's Mr Nobody?

Jenny. Could she have done this somehow? I shook my head. She's only four, I reminded myself. Still, I tiptoed upstairs and checked on the girls. They were sleeping quietly, their breathing regular.

I went back downstairs and stuck the letter in the middle of my maths book. "Mr X" had upset me, but I wasn't going to show the letter to the other club members, or tell them about this either. The Sitter of the Month had to be someone who was in *control*, someone whose sitting jobs always went smoothly. I couldn't risk anyone else knowing about what had happened.

7th CHAPTER

"Yee-ha!" Jackie waved his cowboy hat over his head as he rode around wildly on a broomstick. He was playing rodeo. "Hi-ho, Silver!" he yelled, as he headed into the recreation room.

CRASH!!

Oh, no. I should have seen it coming. Jackie Rodowsky, otherwise known as the Walking Disaster, can barely sit *still* without breaking something. Why hadn't I realized that this game would lead to a catastrophe?

I ran into the recreation room (I had been in the living room with Archie, Jackie's four-year-old brother) to assess the damage. Jackie sat in the middle of the floor, grinning mischievously. "Bet you thought I'd broken something, right?" he asked.

I nodded. "So what happened?"

56

"Nothing," said Jackie. "I knocked over that little table" (he pointed at a red-painted table that lay on its side in a corner of the room) "but it didn't even break!" He sounded proud.

"Great," I said. I should have known that the Rodowskys wouldn't put anything fragile or valuable in the recreation room where the boys played. "But I think it's time to calm down a little. Why don't you come into the living room with Archie and me? We're playing Go Fish."

"Go Fish is a baby game," said Jackie. "Where's Shea? I'll play with him instead."

"Shea's upstairs doing his homework," I said. "He needs peace and quiet. Come and play with me and Archie. We'll have fun." I was *determined* that we'd have fun, since I was still thinking about that Sitter of the Month contest.

I expected Jackie to make a fuss, but he got up and followed me into the living room.

I like sitting for the Rodowskys. I really do. For one thing, dealing with three little red-headed tornadoes is never boring. For another, I like being with Shea, the oldest, since he's about the same age as Jeff and he reminds me of my brother. And Archie is cute. And Jackie—well, Jackie is always a challenge. I've never seen a seven-year-old get himself into so many crazy situations.

For example, the very first time anyone from the BSC met Jackie, he managed to: 1) pull down the shower-curtain rod while trying to hang from it; 2) spill a whole glass of grape juice on the living room carpet; 3) get his hand stuck in a glass jar; 4) fall off his bicycle; and 5) rip his jeans. I think you get the picture.

But he can also be a lot of fun. I remember when I helped him make a robot costume. The activity was full of CRASHes and THUDs, but it was a lot of fun.

Anyway, Jackie followed me into the living room and we settled down on the floor with Archie. While I was gone, Archie had "dealt" the deck of cards into about eight messy piles. He looked pretty satisfied with himself. "Let's play, Dawn," he said.

"Okay," I replied, "but I think we're going to have to start again since there are only three of us. Can you help me?" I reached for one of the piles just as the phone rang. "Be right back," I said as I headed for the kitchen to answer it.

"Hello?" I said into the phone. "Hello?" Nobody was there. I shrugged, hung up, and reached the living room in time to stop Jackie from teaching Archie how to play 52-card pickup. Then I dealt the cards and we started to play.

"Do you have any . . . *threes*?" Archie asked Jackie.

"Um, no," said Jackie. "I mean, Go Fish. I mean, wait a minute. *Threes* did you say? Oh yeah, here." He pulled a card from his hand and tossed it to Archie.

Archie turned to me. "Do you have any—"

The phone rang again.

"Drat," I said. I jumped up and ran for the kitchen. "Sorry, Archie," I yelled over my shoulder. "I'll be back in a sec." I grabbed the phone. "Hello?" I said impatiently. Nobody answered.

All of a sudden a shiver ran down my spine. Was it nobody—or was it *Mr* Nobody? "Hello?" I asked again, but by then, I hardly expected anyone to answer me. I couldn't believe it. Why was this happening? And if it *was* the same Mr Nobody, how did he know to phone me first at the Prezziosos' and then at the Rodowskys'?

I snapped my fingers. Of course. Alan Gray. The most obnoxious boy at school. I remembered hearing about one time— before I joined the club—when he had tormented the members of the BSC for weeks. He'd peeped at our record book to see when and where my friends had sitting jobs, and then he'd made this *exact* type of phone call to those houses.

The thing was, at the time there was also a thief, the Phantom Caller, loose in Stoneybrook. The thief would call houses to find out if anyone was at home. If someone answered, he'd hang up. But if no one answered, he'd rob the house. So of course, Kristy, Mary Anne, Claudia, and Stacey (the original members of the BSC) were terrified. In fact, Mary Anne got so scared that one night while she was sitting at the Thomas's she made all these homemade burglar alarms.

Anyway, Alan Gray eventually got caught, and Kristy found out that he'd been making those calls because he liked her and wanted to invite her to a dance but was too shy to come right out and ask. So instead he made a pest of himself.

And, for whatever reason, he must be doing it again. I shook my head. Oooh, that Alan Gray. I was angry with him, but at least I didn't feel so freaked out about those phone calls since I'd worked out who was making them.

As I was heading back to the living room, I heard the doorbell ring. "I'll get it!" yelled Jackie, and I saw him run out of the living room. I tried to reach the door first, since a responsible sitter doesn't let small children answer the door, but Jackie had a good head start on me.

CRASH! Jackie knocked over the potted palm tree in the front hall as he dashed past it. I stopped to pick it up (luckily no soil had spilled) and Jackie opened the door.

"Nobody's there!" he said, sounding surprised.

You know what? *He* may have been surprised, but I wasn't.

"Look," he said, handing me an envelope. "This was on the doormat. What is it?"

Just then the phone rang again. I rolled my eyes. Jackie took off. "I'll get it!" he cried. I saw him brush by the palm tree again and I ran to catch it before it fell. I stuck the envelope in my back pocket and dashed after Jackie, but I was too late. He'd answered the phone, and by the look on his face I could tell nobody had been on the other end.

"What's going on?" Shea walked into the kitchen. "Is Jackie breaking things again?"

"Everything's fine, Shea," I said.

"No, it's not!" said Jackie. "First I answered the door and nobody was there, and then I answered the phone and nobody was there, either!"

Shea looked at me questioningly, and I shrugged. "It's nothing to worry about," I said.

"But maybe there's a burglar watching the house," said Shea. "I saw this show on TV where—"

"A burglar?" repeated Jackie, wide-eyed. "We'd better call the police." He reached for the phone.

"Wait a minute, wait a minute," I said. "Let's stay calm. Come on into the living room so I can keep an eye on Archie, and we'll talk about it." Jackie and Shea followed me into the living room.

"Where's that letter we got?" asked Jackie, as soon as we'd settled onto the sofa.

"Letter?" I'd almost forgotten about the envelope on the doormat. Now that Jackie reminded me of it, I realized it probably wasn't something I wanted to share with the boys.

"Yeah, the letter," said Jackie. "Maybe it's an invitation to a birthday party."

"We got a letter?" asked Shea.

I sighed. "Here it is," I said, pulling it out of my pocket. I opened it up, and sure enough, it was another note from Mr X, in cut-out letters. *I'm watching you,* it said.

Jackie read it out loud, slowly, because the words were hard to make out, "I'm witch—watching—"

"That's weird," said Shea. "It looks like one of those notes that kid—"

I cut him off before he could say it and scare Jackie. "It's nothing," I said. "Just a practical joke. One of the boys at my school is teasing me."

Shea looked at me closely. "Are you sure we shouldn't call the police?"

"I'm sure," I said. I looked at my watch.

"Anyway, it's past Archie's bedtime, and definitely time for you two to be getting *ready* for bed."

Shea didn't look convinced, but he helped me get Archie into bed, and then he put on his own pyjamas while Jackie brushed his teeth. Jackie was a little spooked, I could tell. And so was Shea, though he didn't want to admit that he was scared.

I tucked the boys into bed, trying to be reassuring. "Your parents will be home soon," I told them. "There's nothing to worry about."

I headed downstairs and straight for the phone book. I was going to put the Mr X/Mr Nobody business to an end right now.

"Let's see," I said to myself. "Graff, Graham, Grant, *Gray*. There it is." I reached for the phone and dialled. When a woman answered, I asked for Alan.

"Alan's not at home, dear," said Mrs Gray.

Aha! I knew it. He was out ringing doorbells and making phone calls.

"He's at a basketball game with his father, in Stamford," she went on. "They won't be home until late tonight."

Hmmm. I thought fast. Even Alan wouldn't go as far as to make *long-distance* prank calls. And besides, if he was in

Stamford, he couldn't have left that letter on the doormat.

"Can I give Alan a message?" asked Mrs Gray. She sounded a little odd, probably because she was wondering why I was being so quiet.

A message? Uh-oh. I wasn't prepared for that. "Um," I said, stalling for time. But I couldn't think of a thing to say. After a couple of seconds that felt like hours, I just hung up. I was so embarrassed! At least I hadn't identified myself.

"Good going, Nancy Drew," I said to myself. "Really slick." I was no closer to identifying Mr X or Mr Nobody than I had been before. The only thing I was sure of was that Mr X and Mr Nobody were the same person. And I was beginning to worry.

8th CHAPTER

Saturday

I hate to say it. I really hate to say it, but maybe sometimes when parents make rules they have good reasons. I mean, plenty of my parents' rules are obviously ridiculous, like the one about not wearing miniskirts, or the one about keeping phone calls short. But maybe, just maybe, the one about not watching horror films isn't all that stupid. Of course, I'd never admit it to them, but for Bessa the rule might make sense. And maybe even for me...

Jessi was sitting that Saturday evening for Becca and Squirt. She loves to sit at night, but she's only allowed to sit for her own brother and sister then. And she doesn't get to do it very often, since her Aunt Cecelia (formerly known as Aunt Dictator) came to live with the Ramseys. When she first arrived, Jessi and Becca thought she was going to drive them insane. She made all these rules and regulations, and she tried to treat both girls like babies. But now they've got used to her, although I think Jessi sometimes still feels she has to prove herself to Aunt Cecelia. She has to act responsibly and be mature and level-headed at all times. How boring.

Anyway, that night Aunt Cecelia had gone to New York to the opera, believe it or not. (Yawn.) And Jessi's mum and dad had been invited to dinner at Mrs Ramsey's boss's house. So Jessi got to sit for Becca and Squirt.

Mrs Ramsey had recently bought new sleeping bags for Jessi and Becca. Jessi planned to use hers for sleepovers, and it was rolled up neatly in her wardrobe. But Becca couldn't bear to put hers away. She loved to spread it out in the TV room and say that she was camping. For the most part, "camping" involved lying on top of the bag while she watched *The Cosby Show*, her favourite.

That night, Becca had decided to let

Squirt camp with her, and they were both inside the sleeping bag. Becca was tickling Squirt, trying to make him give that special gurgly giggle that she loves to hear. Squirt was doing more squealing than giggling, but Jessi could tell by the sound of his squeals that he was having fun. So she didn't try to make Becca stop.

Jessi was busy, anyway, washing the dishes and clearing up the kitchen after dinner. Jessi knew that Aunt Cecelia would be impressed by a spotless kitchen, so she was doing her best to leave it cleaner than it had been when the evening began.

Jessi hummed to herself as she worked. The song was the one that she practises *pliés* to in ballet class, and she's heard it so many times she could sing it in her sleep. Just as she took the last swipe at the worktop by the sink, she heard Squirt squeal one more time. Only this time, it wasn't an I'm-having-tons-of-fun squeal, it was an I-don't-like-this-game-any-more kind of squeal. Jessi dropped the towel she'd been holding and ran for the TV room.

Squirt was still wailing. Becca looked up guiltily at Jessi. "I didn't mean to—" she started to say.

"That's okay," replied Jessi. "I think the Squirtman is just getting tired." Squirt had stopped crying as soon as he heard Jessi's voice, and he was rubbing his eyes in a way that told her he was more than ready for bed. "C'mon, big boy," said Jessi, scooping him up. "Time for bed."

Jessi carried Squirt upstairs and undressed him. Then she changed his nappy and slipped him into a bright purple sleepsuit with dinosaurs on it. She sat in the rocking chair with him and started to hum the ballet song again. But Squirt was having a hard time settling down. He would rub his eyes and cry a little, then smile up at Jessi, rub his eyes and cry some more.

"Becca," called Jessi. "Could you please fill one of Squirt's bottles with water and bring it to me?" Jessi didn't want to give Squirt milk just before bed, since her mum had said it could be bad for his teeth.

"Coming," said Becca, and in a couple of minutes she turned up with the bottle. "Is he almost asleep?" she asked. "There's this film I want to watch with you, and it's starting soon."

"I'll be down in a few minutes," said Jessi, "and then I'll make us some popcorn and we can watch the film."

Becca grinned. "All *right*!" she said. She ran downstairs.

The bottle did the trick, and before long Jessi had tucked Squirt into his cot. She rubbed his back for a minute, saw that he was asleep, and tiptoed out of the room.

Becca was in the kitchen when Jessi came downstairs. "I got out the popcorn maker and the popcorn and even the oil," she said proudly.

"Great," said Jessi. She started to measure popcorn into the popper. "So what's this film you want to watch, anyway?"

Becca didn't say anything. Then, almost under her breath, she said quickly, "*Snake-BoyLooseinSanFrancisco.*"

"*What?*" asked Jessi. "I didn't quite catch that."

"*Snake Boy Loose in San Francisco,*" said Becca, more slowly.

"You're kidding, right?" asked Jessi. "That sounds like one of those films they show on Monster Movie Night."

"It is."

"Becca," said Jessi patiently. "You know we're not allowed to watch scary films."

"Just this once?" asked Becca. "Everybody at school watches them all the time. And Charlotte said she's seen this one before and it's really, really cool."

"Charlotte Johanssen?" asked Jessi. "Her mother lets her watch scary films?"

"Well, not exactly," said Becca. "But once in a while Charlotte watches one anyway."

"Well," said Jessi.

"*Please?*" begged Becca.

"I don't think—"

"Charlotte told me about that Sitter of

the Month contest," said Becca suddenly, changing the subject. "It sounds great." She looked at Jessi out of the corner of her eye. "I don't know *who* I'll vote for."

Jessi got the hint. And even though she knew that she shouldn't, she couldn't resist taking Becca's bait. "Oh, all right," she said. "Just this once. But we're turning it off if it gets too scary. And you have to promise not to tell Mama and Daddy. Or Aunt Cecelia. *Especially* Aunt Cecelia."

Becca was nodding. "Okay, okay," she said excitedly. "I promise. I promise-a-domise-a-vow!"

Jessi smiled. "I think that'll do it," she said. "Now help me bring this stuff into the TV room." They loaded a tray with glasses of apple juice, a bowl of popcorn, and serviettes, and headed for the TV room.

"The film is on channel five," said Becca, heading for the TV and turning it on. "Look, it's just started," she squealed. A ghoulish face was on the screen, with the words MONSTER MOVIE NIGHT written over it in wavery letters.

The film began. At first, it looked sort of funny. There was this boy who had swallowed some chemicals by mistake and turned into a half-boy half-snake creature. He ran round the city scaring women while they hung out their washing or dusted their furniture. Jessi and Becca laughed when a lady jumped about six feet in the air after he'd sneaked up on her.

But then Snake Boy started to become more and more evil. He stalked a teenage girl, watching her as she walked home from school. He even hid in her wardrobe and watched while she did her homework. His plan was to sneak some of the snake-chemicals into her drink so that she'd become a snake, too, and he'd have companionship. Snake Boy was lonely.

The music was really scary during the part when he was hiding in the wardrobe, and Jessi watched, spellbound, as he began to slither towards the table where the lemonade glass was sitting. "Oh, no," she said, under her breath.

Then Jessi heard a whimper. She tore her eyes from the screen and looked at Becca. Becca was sitting covering her ears. Her eyes were squeezed shut.

"Becca!" said Jessi. But Becca didn't hear her. "Becca!" said Jessi, louder this time. Becca looked up at her. Jessi could see that she was terrified. "Okay, that's it," she said firmly. She got up and turned off the TV. "I knew this was a mistake. Come on, let's go to bed."

Becca didn't protest. She held Jessi's hand as they climbed the stairs. "Do you think he's going to turn her into a snake?" she asked.

"No, I'm sure her mother will save her,"

said Jessi, even though she wasn't sure at all. She shuddered. The idea of turning into a snake was so horrible that she couldn't think about it.

Becca had a hard time falling asleep that night, and Jessi had to sit by her bed, reading to her, for quite a while. "I want you to leave the light on," said Becca, before she finally drifted off to sleep. "And leave my door open, too."

Once Becca was asleep, Jessi headed back downstairs, but she did *not* turn the TV on. She collapsed on the sofa, sighing with relief, knowing that she could relax for the rest of the evening since Becca and Squirt were asleep.

Relax? Forget it. What happened next was even scarier than Snake Boy, but Jessi didn't tell us about it for a long time. I think she kept it a secret because she was embarrassed about how frightened she became. Sometimes she's sensitive about being younger than most of the BSC members. She thinks she has to impress us, the same way she has to impress Aunt Cecelia.

Anyway, the first thing that happened was that Jessi got the same kind of phone call I'd been getting. Nobody was there when she picked up the receiver. Then, about ten minutes later, the doorbell rang. When she answered it, nobody was there, either. But on the front step she found a bouquet of flowers.

What's so scary about that? Well, get this. There were no *flowers* on the flowers. It was just a branch of dead, headless stems. Jessi almost screamed when she saw them. And, a note was with them—from Mr X, of course—saying, ***Best wishes from your secret admirer***.

Just as Jessi was recovering from *that* shock, she got another. She heard a piercing scream from the first floor. Her heart was pounding as she dashed up the stairs. She found Becca sitting up in bed, crying. She'd just had a nightmare about Snake Boy.

Becca was still crying when Aunt Cecelia came home.

"What's wrong?" asked Aunt Cecelia.

Becca told all. Jessi couldn't stop her. Of course, Jessi *did* manage to avoid mentioning the phony phone call and the dead flowers. Still, Aunt Cecelia was furious with Jessi, and Jessi was quite cross with Becca for spilling the beans. She knew she'd blown her chance of being Sitter of the Month after *that* disastrous night.

9th CHAPTER

A few nights later, Mary Anne and Mal were sitting together at the Pikes'. Neither of them knew anything about what had happened to Jessi and me. I think we'd each decided to keep quiet about Mr X because of the contest, and because his pranks weren't really *malicious* or anything. But I found out afterwards that Mary Anne and Mal also had a visit from good old Mr X. And it wasn't a friendly visit, either. Here's what happened.

Mr and Mrs Pike had been gone for about half an hour. Mary Anne and Mal were in the midst of supervising dinner, which, as usual at the Pike residence, was a chaotic event. Why? Because Mr and Mrs Pike decided long ago that there was no point in making too many rules for a household of eight kids. They also thought that food was one of the silliest things to make rules about.

They just keep a lot of different kinds of food in the house, and the kids are allowed to eat whatever they feel like eating. It seems to work; those Pike kids are some of the healthiest-looking kids in town.

The only problem is that sometimes the lack of food rules leads to a pretty wild time in the Pike kitchen. Like when the kids went through a phase of eating peanut butter and sardine sandwiches, for instance. (Ugh, ugh, ugh!)

Luckily, that night Mal had decided to avoid the pandemonium that can result when each of her seven brothers and sisters wants to eat something different for dinner. She was going to make a big pot of spaghetti, which is about the only food they all like. But if she thought that her plan would make for a calm, orderly dinner, she was wrong.

Everybody wanted their spaghetti *served* differently. I suppose in a family that big, the kids need to prove themselves as individuals, so they take every opportunity to do so. The triplets, Adam, Byron, and Jordan, wanted to eat their spaghetti out of cereal bowls. But they fought over which *colour* cereal bowl they'd get.

"I want the orange one," said Adam.

"You *always* get the orange one," said Jordan. "I want it this time."

"You two can fight over the orange one," said Byron, "as long as I get the blue one."

"The blue one? I forgot we *had* a blue one," said Adam. He grabbed it out of Byron's hands.

Byron opened his mouth to protest, but Mal stepped in. "You're each getting a white bowl," she said. "Now sit down and eat."

Vanessa, who's nine, was the next Pike to make a fuss over her plate. "Mine's got a crack," she said. "Take it back." Did I mention that Vanessa wants to be a poet? She speaks in rhyme whenever possible. Mary Anne could see that Vanessa's plate wasn't cracked at all—it had just been an excuse for a rhyme—but she gave her a new one anyway.

Then Nicky got into the act. "I want to eat with chopsticks," he said.

Mal looked at him, surprised. "Where did you get *that* idea?" she asked.

"I saw some people on TV doing it," said Nicky. "It looked like fun."

Mal had her doubts that Nicky, who's eight, would be able to eat spaghetti with chopsticks, but she decided to humour him. She knew there was a pair in one of the kitchen drawers (a souvenir from a Chinese restaurant) so she started to look for them.

Meanwhile, Mary Anne was dealing with Margo, who was being very fussy about how she wanted her spaghetti arranged on the plate. "I don't want any of the sauce to

76

touch any of the spaghetti until *I* mix them up together," she said. Poor Mary Anne tried three times to arrange her plate in the way Margo wanted it. Then she gave up and helped Margo serve herself, instead.

And Claire? Claire's only five, and she was just being silly. She'd already been served her spaghetti in her favourite Sesame Street bowl, and she was eating one strand at a time, trying to learn how to suck it in the way the triplets always did. She was having a hard time "capturing" her spaghettis though, and she kept chasing them round her plate, yelling, "Come here, you silly-billy-goo-goo spaghetti!"

Finally, everybody had been served. Mary Anne and Mal collapsed in their seats, exchanging a tired grin. And Nicky started to sing. "The worms crawl in, the worms crawl out—"

"No way, Nicky," said Mal quickly. "Absolutely no singing about worms while we're eating spaghetti. You know Margo will be sick."

Nicky stopped for a minute. Then he started a new song. "Boys are made of greasy grimy gopher guts," he sang, sounding proud to be a boy.

"Uh-uh," said Mallory. "Not that one either. How about no singing at all for a while?"

"No singing, no singing," sang Nicky.

Jordan and Adam joined in. "No singing, no sing—" And then, just as Mal was about to lose her temper, the bell rang. She gladly jumped up from the table and ran to answer the door.

Guess what? Right. Nobody was there. But there *was* a note. From Mr X, of course. Here's what it said: ***Do you like your hamster? If you do, you'd better keep an eye on him.*** Instead of spelling out the word *eye*, a picture of a huge, gruesome eyeball had been glued to the note. It was staring straight at Mal.

"M-Mary Anne?" she shouted from the front hall. "C-can you come here for a minute?"

Mary Anne ran out of the dining room without noticing that Adam was tiptoeing behind her. Mal didn't see him either. "Look," she said, showing Mary Anne the note. "It's probably nothing, right? Just some silly practical joke." She didn't want Mary Anne to see how scared she was. A Sitter for the Month wouldn't get scared so easily.

"Right," said Mary Anne, trying to sound grown-up. "Nothing to worry about at all. But let's make sure the kids don't see it. *They* might get scared." She hoped she sounded calm and reasonable.

At that moment, Adam ran out from behind the coatrack and grabbed the note. "What is it?" he asked. "I want to see." He read the note, and his face turned white. "Somebody's out to get Frodo!" he whispered. "We have to protect him!" And before Mary Anne and Mal could stop him, he ran back to the dining room to tell the other kids.

"Frodo's in danger!" yelled Nicky. "We've got to protect him." He ran upstairs, his brothers and sisters trailing behind him, and took Frodo out of his cage. "I think we should hide him," he said.

"I know," said Jordan. "Let's put him in a shoe box. That way, when Mr X looks in his cage, he won't be there." He ran to his room and got the box from his new supersonic trainers. Adam and Byron helped him punch holes in it for ventilation. Then they placed Frodo in the box (they put a flannel in with him, for a bed), and hid the box on the top shelf of a wardrobe.

Mary Anne and Mallory were helpless. There was no way to stop the kids from trying to "save" Frodo. But they were relieved when the triplets agreed that he was safe in the wardrobe.

Unfortunately, ten minutes later, Vanessa decided that Frodo would be lonely in the dark. "We've got to find a better place," she said. "But where, where? In outer space?"

It was Margo's idea to put the shoe box in the oven. "Nobody will ever look in there," she said, "and we can check on him through the window."

Mal ruined that idea by pointing out that someone might turn on the oven without looking inside first. "We don't want to *cook* Frodo," she said. "We want to save him, right?"

Nicky decided that the best thing to do would be to take turns holding on to Frodo. "That way we'll be right there if someone tries to hurt him," he said. The kids trooped into the living room to hang out with Frodo.

Meanwhile, Mary Anne thought that, just in case, she'd check to make sure the doors and windows were locked. But when she opened the back door to peep outside, she got a nasty shock. Lying on the back porch was a dead mouse!

"Mallory!" she called urgently. Mal came running. "Look," said Mary Anne. "Do you think it's a warning? I'm scared." She was beyond hiding her fear by that time.

"I don't know," said Mal. "I'm kind of scared, too. But we can't let the kids see that we're afraid. Anyway, maybe the mouse was just left there by some cat." She grabbed a broom and swept the mouse off the porch and into the bushes.

Mal and Mary Anne did not have an easy job that night. Since Frodo was out of his cage, he got lost not once, but twice, creating total panic. But eventually all the Pikes were put to bed, and the house was quiet by the time Mr and Mrs Pike arrived home.

Mary Anne and Mallory did a lot of talking that night, and they ended up agreeing to keep the night's events secret from the rest of the BSC, since they thought the story would only scare everybody for no good reason. They convinced themselves that a practical joker was at work, and that there was nothing to worry about.

Right.

By the time Mary Anne got home that night, I was asleep. She went to her room and tried to settle down, and finally, she told me later, was able to get to sleep. But not for long.

In the middle of the night, I woke up suddenly and looked round in the dark. At first I didn't know what had woken me, but as I looked around my dark room I started to hear *scritch scritch! Rustle rustle*! The noises were coming from the secret passage that leads into my room! I was so terrified that I ran into Mary Anne's room and shook her, trying to wake her up.

Boy, did she wake up! She let out a shriek that could have broken glass. I shushed her. Then I locked the door—just in case—and turned on the light. "Mary Anne, it's *me*," I whispered. "I heard a noise in the passage!"

"It's Mr X!" she hissed back. "He's in our house! Oh, my lord!"

"Mr X?" I repeated. "You know about him, too?"

"He was at the Pikes' tonight," she said. She told me the story and then I told her about *my* Mr X experience.

"Why didn't you tell me before?" she asked.

"I don't know," I said. "I suppose because I wanted to be the perfect sitter and win Sitter of the Month."

Mary Anne nodded. "I know," she said. "I was thinking the same thing at first. And Mal probably was, too. We decided not to tell anyone else, but maybe we should. I mean, this is getting pretty scary."

"I don't know," I said. "I still think we should keep it to ourselves. After all, Mr X hasn't really *done* anything yet. Someone probably *is* just teasing us. I'd be pretty embarrassed if that person found out how panicked we'd got over some silly notes."

"Okay," said Mary Anne. "But what about those noises? Do you think Mr X could be in the passage?" She looked scared.

I thought for a moment. "No," I said, "I bet it's just squirrels or something. Nothing to worry about."

But I spent the rest of the night in Mary Anne's room, anyway.

10th CHAPTER

Friday

Friday the thirteenth, that is. And it
was a dark and stormy night, too. Anything
could have happened — and a lot did.
But let me start at the beginning....

Kristy was sitting for the Kormans the night after Mary Anne had sat for the Pikes. She didn't yet know about all the scary things Mary Anne and Mal had gone through, though. Was she about to find out about Mr X herself?

When Kristy left her house, the sky was overcast and the wind was blowing lightly. But by the time she reached the Kormans' (they live just across the street, diagonally opposite the Brewers') she could see that a big storm was developing.

As she rang the Kormans' bell, Kristy noticed that the sky had turned that yellowish-green colour that means a thunderstorm is about to start. The trees in the Kormans' garden were being whipped back and forth by gusty winds, and a few drops of rain had fallen.

"Hi, Kristy," said Mrs Korman when she answered the door. She peered past Kristy into the front garden. "My, it looks like a nasty storm is coming," she said. "I'd better bring my umbrella. Come on in before you get soaked," she said. "Skylar's napping, and—"

Just then Bill, who's nine, ran into the front hall. "Wow, look at the sky," he said. "Pretty creepy. I wonder if Melody knows a storm is coming. She's afraid of thunder." He ran to find Melody.

By the time Kristy had seen Mr and Mrs Korman off, Bill had got Melody all worked up. She's only seven, and she scares easily. "Bill says there's going to be a storm," she wailed to Kristy. "And he says that when there's a storm on Friday the thirteenth, awful things can happen."

Kristy frowned at Bill. "Why are you scaring your sister?" she asked. Then she smiled reassuringly at Melody and said, "Friday the thirteenth is just a superstition. And a storm is just—um, a storm. It'll blow over soon." Kristy had forgotten it was Friday the thirteenth, and she wished Bill hadn't reminded her. She's not exactly superstitious, but—well, *you* know. "I'll tell you what," she went on. "Let's batten down the hatches and make the house all cosy and secure. Then that old storm won't bother us."

"Batten down the *what*?" asked Bill and Melody together.

"The, uh, hatches," answered Kristy, who had never stopped to think what the expression meant. "It has something to do with boats, I think. Anyway, it just means that we'll make sure all the windows and doors are shut and that we're safe inside."

"Oh, okay," said Melody. "But let's do it together, okay? I'm still scared."

So they moved through the house together, checking the windows and doors. The Kormans' house is *big*, by the way. Maybe even bigger than Kristy's.

Just as Kristy and Melody and Bill

reached the landing of the first floor, they heard an unearthly shriek. Kristy told me later that she nearly bit her tongue, she was so scared. Melody, who had been sticking to Kristy like glue, practically jumped into her arms.

"Wh-what was *that*?" asked Bill. His face was white. Teasing Melody seemed to have backfired on him. He'd scared himself as well.

"I don't know," said Kristy. "But it came from *that* direction." She pointed down the hall. She started to walk in the direction the noise had come from.

"No, no," said Melody, trying to hold Kristy back. "Don't make me go!"

Then there was another shriek, and suddenly Bill's face turned from white to pink. He looked embarrassed. "Know what?" he said. "I've just worked it out. It's Skylar!"

Kristy laughed. "I've never heard her shriek quite like that," she said. "I never would have guessed that noise came from a baby." She moved more quickly now towards Skylar's room, hoping that Bill and Melody hadn't noticed how scared she had been. Or if they had, that it wouldn't keep them from voting for her in the sitter contest.

"Skylar has been screaming like that ever since she started teething," said Bill. "My

mum says she sounds like a bantree, whatever that is."

Melody giggled. "Not a bantree," she
said. "A *banshee*. I don't know what it is,
either, but I hope she doesn't scream that
way for long. It hurts my ears." For a
moment, she seemed to have forgotten
about the coming storm.

By then, they'd reached Skylar's room
and Kristy had taken her out of her cot.
"Okay, okay," she said soothingly. "We're
here now, and everything's going to be all
right." Skylar stopped shrieking and
grinned at Kristy. "Now, did we finish
checking the windows?" asked Kristy. "It
sounds like the storm is getting clo—"

Boom! A huge thunderclap echoed over-
head. Melody screamed and tried to
scramble underneath Skylar's cot.

"It's all right," said Kristy. "Thunder
can't hurt you. Let's go to the kitchen and
make some hot chocolate." She herded the
kids downstairs. After she'd settled Skylar
in her bouncer, Kristy started to make hot
chocolate. She hoped it would be soothing.
The storm was getting closer, and Melody
was very, very jumpy.

Just as Kristy was pouring milk into a
pan, another clap of thunder sounded, and
the lights went out.

"Oh, no!" said Melody. She started to
cry. "This is scary," she wailed.

Bill made a spooky sound. "Whooo," he said. "I'm gonna get you!"

"Bill," said Kristy, a warning tone in her voice. Then she thought fast. First she'd have to calm Melody down. Then she'd have to find torches. The house was awfully dark all of a sudden. Kristy thought again about Friday the thirteenth. She felt a chill, and goose bumps rose on her arms.

Then the lights came back on. Kristy put down the milk jug she'd been clutching and gave Melody a hug. "See?" she said. "The lights are on again. Everything's okay."

Melody sniffed. "I hope they *stay* on," she said.

"Hey, do you two know how to play Grandmother's House?" asked Kristy. "You know, the game where the first person says, 'I'm going to Grandmother's house, and I'm bringing some chocolate chip cookies.' And then the second person says, 'I'm going to Grandmother's house, and I'm bringing some chocolate chip cookies and a pair of slippers.' Each person has to remember all the things that are being brought." She hoped the game would distract Melody, and sure enough, it did.

"I know how to play!" said Bill. "Let me start, okay?"

Kristy nodded at him as she handed him a cup of chocolate. "Okay, go ahead," she said.

"I'm going to Grandmother's house," he said, "and I'm bringing a slimy worm!"

"Ugh!" said Melody. "Tell him he can't bring that, Kristy."

"He can bring whatever he wants," said Kristy. "You go next. And you can bring whatever *you* want." She handed Melody a cup of hot chocolate.

"I'm going to Grandmother's house," said Melody, thinking as she spoke, "and I'm bringing a—" (she wrinkled her nose) "slimy worm and . . . and . . . and . . . a cute puppy!" She beamed at Kristy.

"Good!" said Kristy. She sat at the table with her own chocolate and some digestive biscuits for everyone. Skylar was soon gnawing happily on a corner of one of them. "Okay, my turn. I'm going to Grandmother's house, and I'm bringing a slimy worm, a cute puppy, and a giant giraffe!" said Kristy.

The game went on for some time. Bill was in the middle of reciting the list "—a giant giraffe, two mutant turtles, five pairs of supersonic trainers, ten guppies, a purple people-eater—" when Kristy noticed the storm was over. The thunder was just a faint echo in the distance. Kristy heaved a sigh of relief, and the phone rang right by her head. She jumped, surprised by the sound. Then she reached for the phone.

"H-hello?" she asked. Her heart was still pounding.

There was no answer.

"*Hello*?" Kristy asked again. She *hates* getting weird phone calls. "Who's there?"

"Oh, honey," said a voice. "I'm sorry. I didn't hear you the first time. It's me, Mum."

"Hi!" said Kristy. "Boy, you had me scared. What's up?"

"I just wanted to make sure you were okay over there," she said. "Our lights were out for a while, but now they're back on. Did you lose power?"

"We did," said Kristy. "But the lights are back on here, too. Everything's fine. Thanks for calling."

Bill was still finishing the "grandmother" list when Kristy hung up. ". . . an anteater, a box of Jawbreakers, and a pink teddy bear." He grinned triumphantly. "I did it!" he said.

"You did a great job, too," said Kristy. "But guess what time it is?"

"Bedtime, I bet," said Melody.

"That's right," said Kristy. "I'll get Skylar tucked in while you two brush your teeth and put your p.j.'s on."

Bedtime went smoothly, except for a brief encounter with the Toilet Monster, a make-believe creature which used to terrify Bill and Melody. Now they talk about the monster just for fun. Once everybody was settled in bed, Kristy headed downstairs and curled up on the sofa with the book she had brought.

The house was quiet and peaceful. Kristy thought about her Friday the thirteenth nervousness and laughed at herself. "No big deal," she said out loud. "I *knew* it was just a supersti—"

The doorbell rang.

Kristy jumped up. Who could be at the door at such an hour? After a moment of panic, she steeled herself and went to see who it was. She looked through the window first, just to make sure it wasn't a burglar or something.

Nobody was there. Kristy gasped. Then she put the chain on the door and opened it a crack. "Oh!" she said. "You scared me!" It was Mr Papadakis, a neighbour and the father of some kids we sit for. He had bent over to tie his shoelace, which was why Kristy hadn't seen him.

"Hi, Kristy," he said. "I didn't know you were sitting tonight. I just came to get Hannie's raincoat. She left it here this afternoon, and I have a feeling she may need it in the morning."

And that was Kristy's Friday the thirteenth.

11th CHAPTER

"It was *so* embarrassing," said Mallory. She was blushing a deep, deep red. "I was pretty spaced out, I suppose. You know, thinking about loads of things but me. And I actually called Miss McCarthy 'Mum'. Can you believe it?"

"I believe it," I said. "I once did the same thing to my third-grade teacher. I thought I was going to die of embarrassment, but luckily nobody else heard."

We were all in Claudia's room, waiting for our Monday meeting to start. And once we got started talking about embarrassing moments, we couldn't stop.

Claud unwrapped a toffee and popped it into her mouth. "Once I walked into the wrong classroom," she said, laughing, "and the worst thing was that I didn't even realize my mistake until about ten minutes into the class!"

92

We all cracked up. "I think," said Stacey, leaning back in her chair, "that the most embarrassing thing that ever happened to me was when I was out shopping with my mum one day. I bought this great pair of earrings, and then I started talking to the cashier about—oh, I don't know what we were talking about—and anyway, when we'd finished our conversation I waved goodbye, and left without the earrings! I remembered them about half an hour later, and I had to go all the way back to the shop."

"Whoa!" said Kristy, suddenly, pointing at the clock. "Now *I'm* embarrassed. It's five thirty-one and I haven't brought the meeting to order! How about it, everyone?"

The meeting started. Stacey collected subs and reported on how much money was in the treasury. Mary Anne announced that we needed to let her know when our schedules changed. The phone rang twice and we arranged jobs. Then there was a lull.

"You know," said Kristy, "I *did* just remember something embarrassing that happened lately. It was when I was sitting at the Kormans' the other night and Mr Papadakis came to the door. At first I didn't see anybody there, and I almost didn't open the door. Then, when I realized it was him,

I was a little flustered. I must have sounded like a jerk."

"Lucky for you it *was* him, and not Mr X," I said, without thinking. Mary Anne and Mal stared at me.

"Mr X?" asked Kristy. "Who's that?"

Then everybody started talking at once.

"Oh, nobody," I said. (And I wasn't really lying!)

"Oh, we might as well talk about it," said Mary Anne, at the same time. "After all, what's the point in keeping it a secret?"

"I think we need to *do* something about it," said Jessi, simultaneously. "I'm afraid he'll do something worse than just send notes and dead flowers."

"*What* are you all talking about?" asked Kristy.

"I think I know," said Stacey. "I wasn't going to say anything, but I've had some weird experiences lately. Last week when I was sitting at the Perkinses', I got *three* phone calls from someone who just hung up. And then on Thursday, I got this note—" She held out an envelope for us to see.

"Okay," said Kristy. "Notes? Phone calls? What's going on here?"

"You really don't know?" I asked. "Nothing strange has happened when you've been sitting?"

"Nope," said Kristy. "I *thought* last Friday was going to turn out to be strange—Friday the thirteenth and all that—but every time the phone or the doorbell rang, somebody was there. Now *please* explain what's been going on. It sounds serious."

So we each told our stories. And, speaking for myself anyway, every story we heard made Mr X seem creepier and creepier.

I told about my night at the Prezziosos', and about the time at the Rodowskys'. (I even told about phoning Alan Gray's house.)

Jessi told about *her* weird phone call, and then about the bouquet of dead flowers. (Ugh!)

Mary Anne and Mal told about their night at the Pikes'.

Stacey told us more about her experiences.

And then Claud spoke up. "It happened to me, too," she said. "At Charlotte's house. I just thought it was a prank when the phone rang and nobody was on the other end."

Kristy looked round at us. "I can't believe this," she said. "Why didn't any of you *say* anything?" She looked at Mary Anne. "I *really* don't believe you didn't tell me the other day when we were at the shopping arcade together."

Mary Anne looked down at her hands, which were folded in her lap, and sniffed. "I'm sorry," she said in a little voice. "I suppose I just didn't want to worry you."

Then she looked around the room. "No, that's not it," she said. She took a deep breath. "To be totally honest, the reason I didn't tell is because of the Sitter of the Month contest. I didn't want anybody to think I was less than a perfect sitter."

"Mary Anne," said Kristy, "that's ridiculous. We're all very, very good sitters, but *nobody's* perfect. And anyway, the things that happened weren't your fault."

Mary Anne sniffed again. I thought I'd better speak up. "I know what you mean, Mary Anne. I think that's why I kept *my* Mr X episodes a secret, too," I said.

"I can't believe it," said Jessi. "We said we weren't going to get competitive, and look what happened. It was *stupid* not to tell each other. What if Mr X is dangerous? Somebody could have got hurt."

"Well, now the secret's out," said Kristy. "And it's time to start trying to solve this mystery."

"There's one thing *I'd* like to know," said Claud. "Why hasn't Mr X bothered Kristy? She's the only one who hasn't heard from him."

Kristy shrugged. "I'm sure he'll get round to me when he has the chance," she said. "Now let me see that note, Stacey. Does anybody else have the notes she got?"

One of mine was in my pocket. I was wearing the same trousers I'd worn at the

Rodowskys' that night. But Jessi didn't have hers. I gave mine to Kristy and she put it next to Stacey's.

"Let's look closely at these," she said. "Maybe we can work out what they have in common. Is Mr X using certain magazines, for example?" She pored over the notes.

I watched as Kristy studied the notes. A thought was forming in my brain, a thought I really didn't want to be thinking. I tried to push it away, but it wouldn't budge. Kristy was acting very concerned about our troubles with Mr X, "acting" was the word I wondered about. *Was* she just acting? Did she know more than she was letting on? Why *hadn't* she received any notes from Mr X? Was it because—oh, no, I didn't want to think it. Was it because Kristy and Mr X were the same person?

I knew how badly Kristy wanted to be the first Sitter of the Month. I mean, we all wanted to win, but if you knew Kristy as well as I do, you'd know that she can be very, *very* competitive. And because she's chairman of the BSC, she probably thought she absolutely *had* to be the first Sitter of the Month.

"What is it, Dawn?" said Kristy. I realized that she was looking straight at me. I must have been staring at her with my mouth wide open as I thought those terrible thoughts.

"N-nothing," I managed to say, just as

the phone rang. Kristy gave me a funny look, but she dived for the phone. I was incredibly grateful to whoever was calling. I had definitely been saved by the bell. No way was I going to accuse Kristy of anything, especially not in the middle of a meeting.

The call was from Dr Johanssen, who needed a sitter for Charlotte on Friday night. Mary Anne checked the record book. "You've got the job if you want it, Claud," she said. "Everybody else is busy."

"Great," said Claud. "I'll take it." She phoned Dr Johanssen to let her know. "I just hope Mr X doesn't make an appearance," she said, as soon as she'd hung up. "This mystery is making me nervous."

"I don't blame you," said Kristy. "In fact, I wish we weren't so busy right now. If we didn't have so much business, we could double up on jobs so nobody would have to sit alone. I'd come with you on Friday if I didn't have to watch Karen and Andrew."

Hmmmm. Kristy really sounded concerned. She sounded sincere, too. Maybe I'd been wrong. Anyway, how could Kristy have been in our neighbourhood all those times? I felt terrible for even suspecting her, and promised myself not to think about it any more.

Kristy was still looking at the notes. "I can't get any clues from these," she said. "I wish the other ones were here, too. Can you all be sure to bring them with you to the next meeting?"

We agreed.

"In the meantime," she went on, "let's be careful out there."

I giggled. She sounded like a police chief talking to her officers.

"What's so funny?" she asked.

I explained, and everybody else laughed, too. It felt good to laugh. It broke the tension. We'd been getting pretty serious. I mean, what was the big deal? A couple of phone calls, some silly notes. They probably added up to nothing. Maybe Mr X would get tired of his game after a while and leave us alone.

Everybody else seemed ready to let the subject drop, too. After all, we couldn't do much that day. We started to talk about "most embarrassing moments" again, and soon we were laughing so hard we'd forgotten about Mr X.

The meeting was soon over. We hadn't solved the mystery of Mr X, but at least we felt less worried about him.

12th CHAPTER

Fryday

Whoever Mr X is, I wish he would just dissapear off the face of the earth. I mean, even if he is'nt dangerus, or evil, or any of that stuff, the fact is that he's a pest. A reel pane. And I wish he'd stop buging us.

Claud was sitting for Charlotte Johanssen on Friday night. She was feeling sorry for herself, because her best friend Stacey was doing something much, much more glamorous than babysitting. Stacey had gone to visit her father in New York, and Mr McGill had got tickets to a very special event. He was taking Stacey to the world premiere of a new film, and she had the chance to meet the *star* of the film, Rik Devine.

"He's only the most gorgeous hunk ever to walk the earth," muttered Claud to herself as she washed the dishes after dinner with Charlotte. "Why should I be jealous?"

"What?" asked Charlotte. "Who are you talking about?"

"Oh, nobody." Claud sighed. "I mean, nothing. I mean, oh, never mind." She knew she'd better stop daydreaming and pay attention to Charlotte. After all, she *wasn't* in New York, climbing out of a limo while crowds of people stared and cheered. She was in Stoneybrook, and she was babysitting for one of her favourite kids. It was time to come down to earth.

"What can we do *now*?" asked Charlotte. "I'm bored."

Bored? Claudia snapped to attention. Bored kids do not elect their sitter Sitter of the Month. "Well, what would you *like* to do?" she asked.

"I don't know," said Charlotte, sounding a bit whiny.

"Do you want to play Monopoly?" asked Claud. That was a generous offer on her part. Playing Monopoly with anybody can be a slow and tortuous experience, but with Charlotte it's the absolute worst. She's a very *deliberate* kid, and she thinks about each move for about ten minutes, until you're gritting your teeth in frustration. The game can take hours.

"I'm sick of Monopoly," said Charlotte. "It's boring and I never win."

Claudia was relieved, but only momentarily. She still had to come up with something to do. She thought for a moment. "How about if we make cookies?" she asked. Even if they made a mess that she had to clean up later, it would be worth it if baking kept Charlotte entertained.

Charlotte frowned and shook her head. "Mum says I'm supposed to stay away from sweets," she said. "I had two cavities last time I went to the dentist. See?" She opened her mouth and pointed at the silver fillings in her molars.

Claud nodded. "I see," she said. "Okay, how about if we see what's on TV?" she asked. We hardly ever resort to TV to entertain the kids we sit for, but sometimes when we're desperate, we do turn it on. And Claud was getting desperate.

"I already know what's on," said

Charlotte. "And I don't want to watch. It's all stupid programmes tonight."

Claud felt, she told me later, like she was banging her head against a brick wall. Charlotte seemed determined to turn down every suggestion Claud made, no matter what. Then Claud had a brainstorm. "Hey, Charlotte," she said. "I almost forgot! I brought my Kid-Kit with me tonight."

"Yea!" shouted Charlotte, beaming. "Where is it?"

"In the front hall," said Claud. Charlotte ran off to get it, and Claud sat there, shaking her head. Why hadn't she thought of the Kid-Kit earlier? Charlotte *loves* our Kid-Kits.

Charlotte ran back with the box. "This looks really great," she said. "Did you redecorate it?"

Claud nodded. "I got bored with the pink sequins," she said, "so I thought I'd see if my new acrylic paints would work on cardboard."

"It looks really, really, cool," said Charlotte, turning the box this way and that in order to study it. "I love these mermaids here," she said, pointing.

"Thanks," said Claud. "Maybe one day I could bring the paints over and you could try them."

Charlotte's eyes lit up. "*Really?*" she asked. "If you did that I might vote for y—" Her hand flew to her mouth. "Whoops," she said. "I'm not supposed to talk about that, am I?"

Claud smiled. "That's okay," she said. "Your secret is safe with me. Now let's see what's in here," she said, opening the Kid-Kit. A lot of the stuff inside was much too young for Charlotte—blocks and baby puzzles and teething rings and rattles. But Charlotte zeroed in on the books.

"What did you bring this time?" she asked. We all know that Charlotte loves reading and we usually try to get to the library before we sit for her, so we can surprise her with new books. Claud's lucky. Since her mum's a librarian, Claudia gets the latest books delivered right to her room. "Oh, wow," said Charlotte. "A new book by Beverly Cleary!" She held it up. "*Muggie Maggie*," she said, reading the title. Then she peeped inside the book. "It's about learning to write joined up," she said. "Just like we're doing!"

Claud was glad Charlotte was so thrilled with the new book. "Why don't you take it and lie down on the sofa?" she said. "I'll work on my maths homework while you read."

"Oh, no," said Charlotte. "I want you to read *to* me. I love it when people read to me, and Mummy's always too busy."

"Okay," said Claudia, raising her eyebrows. Charlotte wasn't going to let her take it easy that night. Claud realized that she

104

was really going to have to *earn* her Sitter of the Month votes. She opened the book and started to read. Charlotte curled up next to her on the sofa.

Claud found that she was drawn into the story, which was about a little girl who decided she didn't want to learn how to write joined up—because it seemed too hard. Claudia could relate to it.

But after two chapters, Claud's throat started to hurt. It was *hard* to read aloud for a long time. "I've got to stop, Char," she said. "My voice is getting tired."

"Oh, please," said Charlotte. "I can't wait to find out what happens. We can't stop now." She took the book out of Claud's hands. "I'll read to *you*," she said. And she started in on the next chapter. Claud wondered for a minute whether a Sitter of the Month would allow such a thing, but soon she forgot about the contest. She curled up next to Charlotte and happily listened to her read.

Charlotte is a very good reader. Claud said she hardly stumbled on hard words, and only once did she actually stop and ask what something meant. She read two chapters straight through, and then handed the book back to Claud. "Your turn," she said.

So they switched back and forth, sitting on the sofa together. It was a cosy evening, and Claud had forgotten about Stacey's big night out.

And then, just as Claud was about to finish chapter six, the phone rang. She rolled her eyes. "Oh, darn," she said. She was so comfortable on the sofa.

"I'll get it," said Charlotte.

"Okay," said Claud, settling back into the soft cushions. Then she realized that the call might be from Mr X and that Charlotte might be frightened if no one said anything. "Whoa, hold on," said Claudia. "Never mind, Char, I'll get it. You sit down and save our place in the book. I'll be right back."

When Claud picked up the phone and said, "Hello?" there was no answer on the other end of the line. Claudia frowned into the receiver and then hung up. Her peaceful night had been ruined.

She went back to the sofa and tried to concentrate on the story of Muggie Maggie, but she'd lost her concentration. She started to stumble over words that Charlotte would have had no trouble with.

Charlotte gave her a funny look. "What's the matter, Claudia?" she asked. "Who was that on the phone, anyway?"

"Uh . . . nobody," said Claud. "I mean, it was a wrong number. And nothing's wrong. I'm fine."

But Charlotte gently took the book from her hands. "I'll finish it," she said. "I *like* reading to you." She picked up the story where Claud had left off.

Claud looked at the top of Charlotte's head and smiled as she listened to her earnest voice. She was thinking about what a sweet kid Charlotte was, when something caught her attention. She heard a noise at the front door, a rustling noise. Someone was sneaking around outside.

Mr X!

Claudia thought fast. Maybe she could catch him in the act if she tiptoed to the door and flung it open. She didn't even stop to wonder how wise the plan was. She just got up in the middle of one of Charlotte's sentences and ran towards the door.

"Claudia, where are—" Charlotte started to ask, but Claud wasn't listening.

She reached the door and threw it open. "Ha!" she said, but nobody was there. No note, either. And no dead flowers. But *something* was on the steps. Claud couldn't believe her eyes. What *was* that goo that was smeared everywhere? It looked totally disgusting. She turned on the porch light and looked closer. "Oh, yuck!" she said, when she realized what it was. "Baked beans!" Somebody had smeared a couple of tins of baked beans all over the porch.

Claud groaned. How was she going to clean up the mess? And would this episode count against her in the Sitter of the Month contest? As long as Charlotte didn't see the beans, it wouldn't.

But just then, Charlotte poked her head out of the door. "What are you doing?" she asked. "And what's all that mess?"

"Nothing," said Claud. But she soon realized that there was no way she could hide the truth from Charlotte. Of course, Claud didn't tell her about Mr X. She just wrote the mess off as a prank, and Charlotte agreed that it wasn't necessary to tell her parents what had happened. Soon Charlotte was helping Claud scoop up the gooey mess, and then, together, they hosed down the porch, rinsing away every last bean. Claudia crossed her fingers, hoping that the Johanssens wouldn't find baked beans in their shrubbery and wonder what had happened.

As Claudia was working, she was thinking. She wasn't very scared by what had happened, but she was irritated by the inconvenience of having to clean up after Mr X. Until he arrived, the night had been going so well. It seemed to Claudia that the contest and the events with Mr X just had to be connected, but she couldn't work out how or why.

13th CHAPTER

I was feeling a bit down as I walked to the Newtons' house the next Tuesday afternoon. One weekend and one meeting later, the BSC was no closer to solving the mystery of Mr X. We didn't have *any* clues, or *any* suspects, or anything. And, just when we wanted to be doing the best sitting we were capable of, Mr X was making that impossible.

But I had arranged a sitting job with Jamie and Lucy that afternoon, and I resolved to do my best to forget about Mr X and just make sure the kids had a good time. Not so much because I wanted to win that Sitter of the Month contest (although I'm sure I don't need to tell you that I *did* want to win), but because I felt those kids deserved my full attention.

After I'd rung the Newtons' doorbell, I took a deep breath and stood up straight.

Concentrate, I told myself. And then Jamie flung the door open and started to tell me about his new Spiderman doll, and Lucy was crying because she needed a new nappy and a bottle, and Mrs Newton was apologizing because she was running late and "had to dash," and I had no time to give Mr X another thought.

I admired Jamie's new doll and changed Lucy's nappy. Then I made up a bottle for Lucy and a snack for Jamie (peanut butter and honey sandwich on toast—he loves it).

Jamie is one of my favourite kids to sit for. First of all, he's four years old, which is a great age. He's just beginning to learn all kind of things about the world, and he's full of excitement and curiosity. Second, he's a total sweetheart. He's very affectionate and hardly ever cranky, and he *adores* his baby sitter. No sibling rivalry there!

It's not hard to see why he loves Lucy so much. She's a very lovable baby. She's got fine, dark hair and beautiful deep blue eyes, and she's learned that smiling at people is guaranteed to make them smile back. She's got the sweetest smile.

"Know what?" asked Jamie as I cleared up after our snack. "I had to stay home from nursery school yesterday."

"Oh, really?" I asked. I happened to know that Jamie had been at nursery school the day before, because Mrs Newton had mentioned it when she'd phoned to arrange this job. But I also know that Jamie calls anything in the recent past "yesterday", and anything in the future "tomorrow". So I thought he was talking about a day last week when Mrs Newton said he'd had a touch of flu. "Were you feeling sick?" I asked.

He nodded, his eyes wide. "I felt *terrible*," he said.

"Did you throw up?" I asked. When you're a kid, throwing up is the worst. (Not that it's much fun once you're older.)

"No," said Jamie. "But I *feeled* like it."

I held back a giggle. He looked so serious. "But you're all better now, right?" I asked. "And ready to have some fun today?"

"Right!" he yelled. He jumped out of his booster seat and ran to Lucy's high chair. "Come on, Lucy-Boosy-Goosie! Finish your bottle so we can play!"

Lucy grinned at him, and let her bottle drop to the floor.

"I think she's finished," I said. I picked up the bottle and lifted Lucy out of her high chair. "Now," I said to Jamie. "How about if we go outside and play on your swing set?" I'd noticed Jamie seemed especially full of energy that afternoon, and decided he needed to work some of it off.

"Yeah!" said Jamie. Then he paused for a moment, and a frown passed over his face. "I mean, um," he said, looking as if he'd had second thoughts. "Can we play in the *front* garden instead?" he asked.

"Of course," I said. "Whatever you want." Usually Jamie loves to be pushed until he's swinging "way high", but if he wasn't in the mood, that was fine with me. "What shall we do?"

"Can you help me practise my catching?" he asked. "When softball season starts I want to be the best catcher on Kristy's Krushers."

That's the name of the softball team Kristy coaches. Jamie's one of the youngest kids on the team, and I know he tries really hard—but he's afraid of the ball. He ducks every time it comes near him. "Of course we can," I said, "as long as Lucy doesn't mind sitting in her bouncer and watching us." I was pretty sure she'd cooperate, at least for a while. Lucy loves watching Jamie do things.

"All *right*!" said Jamie. "I'll go and get my mitt and the softball."

Suddenly I had a great idea. "Wait a second, Jamie," I said, "I think I've got something in my Kid-Kit that we can use instead of a softball." I found my Kid-Kit, which I'd left on a table in the front hall, and rummaged around in it. Sure enough, Jeff's old Wiffle ball was still in there. I thought that if we used *it* for practice, maybe Jamie could get over his fear of the ball. After all, a Wiffle ball can't really hurt you.

We headed outside and I settled Lucy in her bouncer, in the shade of a big tree. I gave her some toys to play with: a doll, some plastic rings, and an empty plastic peanut-butter jar that she seemed to love. Then I started to toss the Wiffle ball to Jamie, and he worked hard on his catching. I threw him high ones, low ones, hard ones, and soft ones, and he did his best to catch every one. Not once did he duck away from the ball, the way he usually does when he's playing softball.

"You know," I said to him after ten or twenty throws, "I think your catching really improves when you stop worrying about the ball hitting you."

"I know," he said. "I'm not afraid of *this* old ball." He looked at the Wiffle ball in his mitt. "So all I have to do in a real game is pretend that the softball is a Wiffle ball, right?"

"That ought to do it," I said. I was happy that my idea had worked, and that Jamie had learned something from our practice. "Now, how about if we take a break from catching and take Miss Lucy for a walk? I think she's getting bored." I pointed to Lucy, who was starting to fuss a little.

"Of course!" said Jamie. "Can I push the bug—" He stopped in mid-sentence. "Oh, no," he said. "We can't go for a walk. We're supposed to stay in the house until Mel comes by."

113

"Mel?" I asked, raising my eyebrows.

Jamie put his hand over his mouth. "I wasn't supposed to tell," he said. "Never mind."

"Jamie," I said, a warning tone in my voice. "Why is Mel coming by?"

Jamie looked caught. "He's—he's doing a secret babysitting check on you. He said it's for the contest. He said I would be a big help if I made sure we stayed at home today." He glanced up at me. "Hey, maybe you'll win, Dawn," he said. "You're a *great* babysitter."

I smiled at Jamie. "Thanks." But as I smiled and tried to act normally, my mind was racing at about three million miles an hour. Mel Tucker doing secret babysitting checks? Something didn't fit. I tried to think. What was wrong with this picture? And then I knew. Don't ask me how I knew, but I just *knew*. Mel Tucker was Mr X.

It didn't even make sense. I had no idea why Mel would be out to get the members of the BSC. I didn't know what purpose he might have for sending us nasty notes, making weird phone calls to us, or doing any of the other things Mr X had been doing. But I was sure. And I was almost positive that if Jamie and Lucy and I hung around the Newtons' house for the rest of the afternoon, *something* would happen to prove me right.

114

"Okay," I said. "Jamie, it doesn't matter that you told. Your secret's safe with me."

He smiled. "You won't tell Mel?" he asked.

"I won't," I said. "And let's forget about that walk and just stay close to home. I think Lucy might be ready for a nap, anyway." She was rubbing her eyes and looking sleepy. I scooped her up and grabbed whatever toys I could find. She'd scattered them pretty well. Jamie picked up the bouncer.

"I can carry this," he said proudly.

"I'm impressed," I said. "You're getting to be *such* a big boy, and you're such a good helper." Jamie beamed and followed me into the house.

I settled Jamie in the playroom with his Bert and Ernie puzzle and headed upstairs with Lucy. It didn't take long to put her down for a nap. She must have been awfully sleepy. Back downstairs, Jamie had already finished the puzzle I'd given him and started on another.

"This Big Bird one is harder," he said. He leaned over the puzzle, concentrating hard. I could see that he didn't want any help. I leaned back in my chair, thinking about my idea that Mel Tucker = Mr X. Why? Was he just doing these things as pranks? Why was he focused on us baby-sitters? There was so much I didn't know.

"There!" said Jamie, putting the last piece in. "I got it!"

"Good job," I said. "Now, what do you—" Just then, the doorbell rang. Aha. I had a feeling it *wasn't* Avon calling, if you know what I mean. I made a mad dash for the door, hoping to catch Mr X in the act, but he was too quick for me. By the time I threw the door open, nobody was there. Nobody, that is, except Lucy's doll. And Lucy's doll was missing her head.

"Ugh!" I cried, before I could catch myself.

"What?" asked Jamie, from behind me.

"Oh, nothing," I said, trying to calm myself. "Why don't you go back inside? I'll be there in just a second."

"But I've finished my puzzle," he reminded me.

"Oh, right," I said. "Well, why don't you choose a book for me to read to you?" I thought that would take a couple of minutes. Jamie went off to find a book, and I ran into the garden looking for the doll's head. I didn't want Mrs Newton to come home and find Lucy's doll decapitated. (That means with her head chopped off, in case you're wondering.) But the head was nowhere to be seen.

I spent the rest of the afternoon trying to distract Jamie in order to search for the doll's head, but the only result was a confused Jamie and a frustrated me. Finally

I stuck the doll into the overflowing toy basket in the playroom, hoping Mrs Newton wouldn't notice it.

When I got home that day, I ran straight into Mary Anne's room and told her what Jamie had said about Mel. Then I told her about the doll. "So, don't you see?" I asked. "It's obvious that Mel is Mr X."

"I'm not so sure," said Mary Anne slowly. She's always so cautious. "But I can see why you're suspicious. What we have to do is make a plan. We have to catch Mel in the act—with witnesses. Then we'll know for certain."

"You're right," I said. "We need a plan." We thought for about two seconds, and then, practically at the same moment, we both said, "Let's phone Kristy."

Kristy was excited when she heard my story. I felt terrible that I had ever even *suspected* that she might be Mr X. What a ridiculous idea *that* had been! She declared that the next day's meeting would be an emergency meeting, and that our main goal would be to make a plan to catch Mel. Mr X's days were numbered.

14th CHAPTER

The emergency meeting was one of our best ever. I have to say that while the BSC has been through some pretty rough spots—times when the club *almost* broke up—we really *can* be good in a crisis. We came up with a plan, and what a plan it was. Guaranteed to catch Mr X in the act!

And for once, the great idea wasn't Kristy's. In fact, it was—guess whose— mine! Then Kristy and the others added some terrific finishing touches, and by Saturday night, we were ready.

For several days, I spread the news about a sitting job I had lined up for Saturday night. Supposedly, this cousin of mine was going to be visiting, and I would be taking care of him at my house while my mum and Mary Anne's dad went out with his parents. I let it be known that I'd be alone, too. The story was that Mary Anne had a sitting job across town.

I told *lots* of people my story because I wanted to be sure Mel heard about the "job". This was one time that I really wanted Mr X to pay me a visit! I told Gabbie and Myriah Perkins when I saw them at the library. I told Nicky Pike, and I also told the triplets. I told Jamie Newton when I saw him at the supermarket with his mum. And I told Becca Ramsey, since she answered the phone one night when I phoned to speak to Jessi. None of the kids seemed to think my telling them the story was at all strange, which was lucky. I didn't want anyone getting suspicious. But I *did* want to be sure that Mel got the news.

You see, I happen to know that Mel knows about the secret passage in my house. *All* the kids in the neighbourhood think it's the coolest thing. I had a feeling Mel might try to use that secret passage to scare me out of my wits! In fact, I was sort of wondering if he'd already tried that, the night Mary Anne came home scared from the sitting job at the Pikes'. I'd definitely heard some weird noises that night, but I wasn't *sure* Mel had made them. After all, we'd heard those noises pretty late.

Anyway, if Mel did what we thought he'd do, he would enter the passage through its opening in the barn. And once he was in there, we'd have him trapped!

My mum and Richard had plans that night, and they left at about seven-thirty. At seven forty-five, I heard a knock on the back door. "Mary Anne!" I hissed. (She was at home, of course. Her sitting job across town was just part of the story.) "Quick, let them in!" I was in the front room, checking to make sure the curtains were drawn so nobody could see in.

When Mary Anne answered the door, she found Kristy, Claud, Stacey, Jessi, and Mal collapsed in a heap of giggles on the back porch. I ran into the kitchen when I heard them come in. "Hey, you lot, be quiet!" I whispered. Of course, nobody heard me. "Hey," I said, a little more loudly. "C'mon, this is serious business tonight!"

They only giggled more. I shook my head, trying to look disgusted. But before I knew it, I was giggling, too. I suppose we had a case of nerves, and giggling was a good way to get rid of some of the tension we were feeling. For a few minutes, we couldn't stop laughing. Every time we started to calm down, someone would say, "Okay, now, shhhhh!" with her finger over her lips. And that, for some reason, would set everybody off again.

Finally we managed to get a grip on ourselves. We sat around the kitchen table for a quick last-minute meeting on strategy. I passed around a bowl of crisps as Mary Anne poured lemonade for everyone.

"Okay," I said. "Does everyone know what to do?" We each had a role to play in the plan we'd made.

My friends nodded.

"All right," I said. "Now, I've got the check-list here," I went on, pulling out a clipboard. "Let's run through it quickly." I heard a snort from across the table, and I looked up to see Stacey stifling a giggle.

"I'm sorry," she said. "It's just that you sound like some four-star general or something. All this planning, just to catch little Mel Tucker in the midst of a prank."

Before I could say anything, Kristy gave Stacey a Look. "I for one think Dawn is doing a great job," she said. "You *have* to plan these things, otherwise you can't be sure you'll succeed."

"Hear, hear," said Claudia. "And we definitely want to succeed. I don't want that little pest getting away with *one more* prank. I want to see Mel caught."

"But what if it's not Mel?" asked Mary Anne in a small voice. "I mean, we don't have *proof* that it's him. I feel bad that we've just gone and decided that Mel is Mr X. It's as if he's been found guilty without a trial."

"Mary Anne," I said, trying to be patient. "We've been over this before, remember? It doesn't *matter* if it's not Mel. This plan we've made will catch Mr X in the act, whoever he—or she—is. It might be Mel, or it might be anyone. It might be the Queen of England!"

"The Queen of *England*?" repeated Claudia. "Somehow I doubt that she's sneaking around Stoneybrook ringing door-bells!"

"Yeah," said Mal. "I mean, Princess Di, maybe. But the Queen? Never."

We cracked up again. But before the giggling could get out of hand, I held up the clipboard. "Okay, c'mon," I said. "Let's get this done. We'll organize the barn squad first."

"Barn squad?" asked Mary Anne. "Oh, I suppose that's me, Kristy, and Stacey, right?"

"Right," I answered. "Now, let's double check on the signal. When I nod my head, what does that mean?"

"Um . . ." said Mary Anne. "It means 'yes'."

"Mary *Anne*," I said.

"Okay, okay," she said. "When you nod your head, it means we should head for the barn."

"Good," I said. "Now, let's do an equipment check. Torches?"

"Check," said Kristy.

"Polaroid camera?"

"Check," said Stacey.

"Film?"

"I've got it," said Mary Anne.

"You're supposed to say 'check'," I said.

"Check," she said.

"Okay, load the camera," I said. "Now, how about the house crew? Everybody ready?"

"Yup," said Jessi.

"Check," said Mallory.

"Ready," said Claudia. "I've got our team's camera, and it's loaded and ready."

We didn't know if photos would be necessary, since there would be so many witnesses, but we thought that a snapshot of Mr X caught in the act would be definite proof. Nobody could argue against a picture.

"I think we're all ready," I said. I sort of wished my checklist was longer. I was finding out that being in charge was fun. No wonder Kristy likes being chairman. On the other hand, I wouldn't like to have that kind of responsibility *all* the time. I wasn't crazy about the tense feeling and the stomachache that went with it. I grabbed a wholewheat cracker and ate it, just to keep my mind off things.

"What do we do now?" asked Jessi.

"We wait," I answered. "I bet Mr X will arrive any minute."

Any minute? We sat there for almost an hour. At first we talked, just to pass the time. We talked about who our "dream boyfriend" would be, and about what high school was going to be like, and about who in history we'd like to have been. That kind of thing. We'd been over it a million times before, but it's always fun.

After a while, though, we ran out of things to say (something that doesn't happen very often) and we just sat quietly, waiting for Mr X to show up.

It was a good thing, because when Mr X did arrive he started out almost silently. I nearly missed the sound. But there it was. Footsteps. Very *light* footsteps, in the spot where the secret passage goes by the kitchen. I put my finger to my lips. "Shhh," I whispered, just in case. I gestured towards the wall and raised my eyebrows. Then I started to tiptoe out of the kitchen, hoping the others would remember that they were supposed to follow me.

They did. We tiptoed upstairs in single file, making an amazingly tiny amount of noise. There was no giggling, and nobody tripped or knocked over a table. I was proud of us.

By the time we reached my room, Mr X had begun his show. *Scritch scritch*! He ran his nails over the wall. *Whooooooooo*! He moaned like a forgotten soul. *Hee hee hee*! He laughed like an evil spirit.

It was kind of funny, until I realized that if I really *had* been in the house alone, I would have been scared to death. The thought made me angry all over again. It was time to catch Mr X in the act. I looked at Mary Anne, Kristy, and Stacey, and slowly nodded my head. They nodded back seriously. Then they turned and left the room.

I checked my watch. Mary Anne and I had timed the trip from my room to the barn, and we'd decided to allow two and a half minutes for it. When my friends left, it was eight thirty-four.

I gave them until eight thirty-seven, just to be sure. Then I looked at Mal, Jessi, and Claud with my eyebrows raised. "Ready?" I said, moving my lips without making any noise.

They nodded.

I walked to the door of the secret passage and, without pausing, threw it open.

"Aha!" I shouted, along with Mal, Jessi, and Claudia.

Mel Tucker stared at me with big, round eyes. He looked terrified. For a second I thought he was going to cry. Instead, he turned and ran back down the passage. I stuck my head into the passage, hoping to hear what happened at the other end. Sure enough, it wasn't long before I heard a faint "Aha!" echo through the corridor.

I ran downstairs with the others behind me, and in a minute we met up with the "barn squad", plus Mel, in the kitchen. None of us had remembered to take a Polaroid of Mr X, but it didn't matter. Mel was obviously the guilty party. He was standing by himself in the middle of the room, looking furious.

"I didn't do anything!" he said, sticking out his lower lip. "I was just—"

"Yes?" I asked. "You were just *what*?"

Mel seemed to be thinking hard, but he couldn't work out how to explain what he'd been up to. He bit his lip, and I saw tears well up in his eyes.

I had been sure that when I caught Mr X I would give him a piece of my mind. I was going to tell him off for scaring us and for making a pest of himself. But when I saw Mel crying, I wasn't angry any more. He wasn't an evil mastermind. He was just a little kid with a dirty, tear-streaked face, and a hole in his jeans.

I walked over to him and got down on my knees. "It's okay, Mel," I said. I opened my arms, but he held back. He looked embarrassed. "It's okay," I repeated. He took a step towards me and then he flew into my arms. I gave him a big hug.

15th CHAPTER

Wow. *The Capture of Mr X.* It would have made a great film. But its ending was more sad than exciting. When Mel's tears had finally slowed down, Kristy and I walked him home. On the way, he confessed to everything.

Well, not quite everything. Mel insisted that he didn't know a thing about the dead mouse Mary Anne had found on the Pikes' back doorstep. "Yucko," he said. "I like *live* mice, but I wouldn't pick up a dead one." He also denied being in the passage later that same night. "Must have been a squirrel," he said.

Kristy and I were gentle with Mel. I think she felt the same way I did—that he was just a troubled little boy and that he needed help more than anything. We knew that *he* knew that what he'd done was wrong. He answered all our questions about how he'd pulled his pranks. Then, just as we turned the corner onto his street, I asked him one last question.

"Why did you do it, Mel?"

He looked at me and his eyes filled with tears all over again. "Because you lot got me into trouble, that's why," he said.

"What do you mean?" I asked.

"Mrs Hobart phoned my parents and said her babysitter had told her that I was teasing her kids. So what if I was? It was no big deal. And it wasn't anybody else's business."

"Hold on there," said Kristy. "It *is* a big deal. You have to learn to stop bullying kids who are different from you."

"That's what my father said," said Mel, hanging his head. "He was really angry. So was my mum. They said I was grounded for two months!"

"So you've been sneaking out of the house in order to be Mr X?" I asked. "Now you're going to be in even more trouble."

Mel nodded. "I know," he said. "But that Sitter of the Month Contest gave me the perfect chance. It was so easy to find out where you lot were babysitting. The other kids were happy to tell me, as long as they thought it would help their favourite sitters win." He looked miserable. "But now I've really messed up. Mum said that if I didn't start to behave properly I might have to talk to a sie-sike—"

"A psychiatrist?" suggested Kristy. She glanced at me. "You know, Mel, that might not be so bad. A psychiatrist is like a doctor for your feelings. He can help you work out why you're feeling sad or angry, and help you learn how to feel better."

I smiled over Mel's head at Kristy. She'd put that well!

Mel looked hopeful. "Really?" he asked. "I didn't know that. I thought the sike-sike-eye—the feelings doctor was just going to punish me."

Poor Mel. He seemed like a scared little kid who didn't know how to deal with feeling angry. And when he knocked on the door of his house, he looked more scared than ever.

His parents were angry at first, but then they calmed down. When we explained the situation, his mum said, "Oh, *Mel*!" And his dad looked very stern. But then they knelt down to give Mel hugs. "You're really feeling terrible, aren't you?" asked his mum. "I think it's time for us to have a talk." We watched as they walked hand-in-hand towards the sofa. Mel turned and gave us a tearful smile and a wave. Then Mr Tucker walked us down the street and to the corner.

"Mel is having some problems these days," he told us. "We've tried everything, but we don't know how to help him any more. We've been so worried about him.

Mrs Tucker has heard about a wonderful child psychiatrist, and I'm going to phone her and make an appointment first thing on Monday morning. Maybe Mel can get the help he needs."

Mr Tucker looked sad.

"Mel's basically a sweet kid," I said. I wasn't sure if I should say anything at all, but I couldn't help myself. "He doesn't mean to hurt anyone's feelings when he teases. I'm sure everything will work out."

Kristy and I walked back to my house together that night, talking about Mel. I was sure the psychiatrist would be able to help him work things out. Just before we got to my house, I stopped and turned to Kristy.

"There's something I have to tell you," I said. "For a while I thought you might be Mr X."

"*What*?" Kristy asked. "Why would I do something like that?" Before I could answer, she'd guessed. "Oh, because of the contest, right?"

"Right," I answered. "Kristy, I am so, so sorr—"

She waved her hand. "Don't worry about it," she said. "I'll bet some of the others thought so, too. I suppose it *did* look pretty suspicious, since Mr X never bothered me."

"Now we know why," I said. "Mel could never have got over to your neighbourhood on his own. And that's where all your jobs have been recently."

That night we celebrated the capture of Mr X with a sleepover at my house. (We'd planned the sleepover during our emergency meeting.) By the time Kristy and I got home from the Tuckers', the others had already ordered pizza. And by the time Kristy and I had told about walking Mel home, the pizzas had arrived.

We sat at the kitchen table, and each pulled a piece of hot, cheesy pizza from the box. "May I propose a toast?" I asked, before anybody could take a bite. "To the BSC," I said. "The best Mr X-Busters in the state of Connecticut!"

"And to Mr X," said Kristy, quietly. "May he be a happier boy soon."

We raised our pizza in the air and pretended to click the slices together. Then we proceeded to pig out.

The next Monday afternoon, we were halfway through our club meeting when we heard a knock at Claud's bedroom door.

"Who is it?" asked Kristy.

An explosion of giggles was her only answer. I opened the door. A crowd of kids were in the hallway, looking at me with mischievous smiles. Jamie Newton was there, and Nicky Pike, and Charlotte and Becca. I saw David Michael and Jackie

Rodowsky. The Pike triplets were on their way up the stairs, and Adam was shouting "Wait for us!" Even Zach Wolfson was there.

The other club members had got up to see who was at the door, and Kristy leaned over my shoulder. "What are you kids up to?" she asked.

"We came to tell you who won the Sitter of the Month Contest," said Byron. He was panting from running up the stairs.

The contest! We'd forgotten about it. Solving the mystery of Mr X had come to be much more important.

"Mel tried to mess everything up, but we decided to vote anyway," said Adam, taking up where Byron left off, "and we knew you'd want to know the result right away."

"So?" asked Kristy. "Who won?"

"Yeah," I said. "Who won?"

I could almost feel each of the club members holding her breath. Suddenly I felt that I wanted to win. I really, really did.

"Well," said Nicky. "We all voted for our favourite sitter. And you know what? There was a tie!"

"A tie!" I asked. "Between who?" I thought Kristy had to be one of the top two. But who was the other?

I didn't have any time to wonder.

"Between *all* of you!" yelled Jackie.

"A seven-way tie!" shouted Jordan.

"You're *all* our favourite sitters," said Becca and Charlotte together.

I turned to look at the other club members. Mary Anne had tears in her eyes (that's Miss Sensitive for you) but everyone else was grinning. I held up my hand for a group high-five. "Congratulations!" I said. "And *yea* for the Sitter of the Month!"

You Be The Jury
by *Marvin Miller*

Did Mr Rogers fake his burglary to claim the insurance money?
Is Stanley Woot's last will and testament a fake?
Did John Goode shoot his business partner by accident – or was it attempted murder?

Ten intriguing courtroom mysteries are played out before you. Examine each case, study the evidence, then make your decision. The final verdict is up to you!

You Be The Jury II
by *Marvin Miller*

Here we have twenty more intriguing courtroom mysteries for you to solve.

Which one of the identical Lee twins vandalised Farmer Foley's chicken coup?
Did Brenda Taylor deliberately set fire to her jewellery shop so she could claim the insurance money?

Examine each case, study the evidence, then make your decision. The final verdict is up to you!

You Be The Jury III
by *Marvin Miller* illustrated by *Harry Venning*

Order in the Court!

The court is now in session and *you* are the jury!
In these ten mysterious cases *you* must examine the evidence, *you* spot the clues, and *you* decide the verdict – Guilty or not guilty.

You Be The Detective
by *Marvin Miller*

Can YOU solve the crime?

Seven baffling crimes have been committed, and YOU are the detective. You have to visit the scene of the crime, question the suspects and piece together the clues.

Who Dunnit?
by *Marvin Miller* illustrated by *Harry Venning*

A brilliant book for all budding detectives, with picture puzzle crimes to solve, a complex collection of codes to crack, hints on how to search for clues – in fact, everything you need to become a supersleuth.

HORRIBLE HISTORIES
History with the nasty bits left in!

The Awesome Egyptians
by *Terry Deary* and *Peter Hepplewhite*

The Awesome Egyptians gives you some awful information about phabulous Pharaohs and poverty-stricken peasants – who lived an awesome 5,000 years ago!

Want to know:
★ which king had the worst blackheads?
★ why some kings had to wear false beards?
★ why the peasants were revolting?

In this book you'll find some foul facts about death and decay, revolting recipes for 3,000-year-old sweets, how to make a mean mummy, and some awful Egyptian arithmetic.
History has *never* been so horrible!

The Terrible Tudors
by *Terry Deary* and *Neil Tonge*

The Terrible Tudors gives you all the grizzly details of Tudor life for everyone – from cruel kings and queens, to poor peasants and common criminals.

Want to know:
★ some terrible Tudor swear words?
★ about terrible Tudor torture?
★ why Henry VIII thought he'd married a horse?

Read this book to find some foul facts, some horrendous beheadings, a mysterious murder, some curious quizzes and gruesome games.

History has *never* been so horrible!